The Cusp of Something

The Cusp of Something

stories

Jai Clare

LASTIC
PRESS

ISBN number: 978-0-9553181-3-9

Printed and bound by Biddles, King's Lynn, Norfolk

Cover painting by Ray Donley (www.raydonley-online.com)
Cover layout by Dean Harkness
Typeset by Andrew Hook

Published by:
Elastic Press
85 Gertrude Road
Norwich
UK

elasticpress@elasticpress.com
www.elasticpress.com

I owe many thank yous to people for help and encouragement over the years but I can only name a few here so many thanks first to Andrew Hook and Elastic Press, thanks to Paul Smith my ex art teacher who got me writing in the first place, to everyone at Zoetrope who have been invaluable, particular thanks to Wendy Vaizey and Mary McCluskey, also to Alan Roche. Wish I could name you all! Thank you.

Table of contents

Balloons

"But," I said, "what if we fall in love with someone else?" You said, "We'll talk about it when it happens."

So I moved across oceans for you, to a large brick building in a squashed high-rise city full of the homeless, the carefree, and the stressed. Here I sat every night in an apartment large and airy, with gigantic views of steel buildings and distant hills dwarfed by the metallic glintings of the city, and thousands of night-lights consuming the air, and waited for you. I loved waiting for you. I would think about you as I dressed, my skin tingling as I put on the clothes you loved so much. I adored your tenacious ambition, the twist of your slightly crooked nose, your eyelashes full of city grit, and your dark parted hair, flecked with highlighted grey.

You worked down the street. I could just see your building from mine. I knew when you got to work. I knew when you left. I knew what you had for lunch. I knew what jokes made you laugh uncontrollably.

During the day I discovered the city: tiny roads leading to murmuring cafés, bookshops, and delis full of spices and incense sticks hanging from the ceiling. I loved to walk around the city, to discover which area merged into another. I knew the streets better than you did. I told you this and you were surprised, as you were surprised when I bought you

1

rare vinyl records from shops you never knew existed. Your face would light up when you visited my apartment every night straight from work to find a new selection waiting for you. You said your window looked across to large buildings full of important people. You could see them moving, making calls.

You were there when the big balloon descended.

The sky that Sunday was full of colours: blue and red and patches of green and some yellow between the metallic points of buildings, and words on top of colours. Words flung across that tepid, uncertain morning blue like a ticker tape of news. A festival of balloons. I cried when I opened the blinds and saw them there. Balloons. Balloons flitting between harsh corners of brick and glass. Balloons by themselves; balloons with messages; balloons attached to baskets; people in baskets throwing out balloons for children: red and yellow and blue taking to the sky and floating across windows like confetti. I watched as people came to their windows and opened the shutters – bleary-eyed people in strange garbs of pyjamas and t-shirts and sometimes nearly nothing. The sight of the balloons filling the skies made them forget their nakedness. They smiled; they gasped; they hurled open their windows; they tried to grab the smaller balloons. They read the words on the side of them.

You told me you saw the big balloon slowly fall. You were standing at the window drinking coffee as it came into view. First the basket. People laughing, then worried as they realized they were falling. Then the fabric filling the window view. You stood there gazing in wonder. I imagine they tried to save themselves. I see them calling out to you. I see their hands grabbing at you to help them, plundering every emotion you had. You never said why you were at work on a Sunday. The day had hardly begun but you were at your desk instead of in my bed. The balloon was blue and red, patches of blue and red. It was huge. If you'd reached out to touch it your hand would have vanished amongst the colours. It seemed to descend slowly past your window. You couldn't believe how slowly it fell, as if a whole century passed whilst the folds of fabric fluttered and moved in on itself. Hollows appeared in the fabric, great dents, like craters. Mountains rose; red and blue mountains rising like atolls.

You came to me later, mostly silent, easy to manoeuvre. You said, "I can never love again. I am emptied of love." A whole ocean washed between us. You seemed to vanish into the water, under the floorboards into the hole that emerged and swallowed you. I stood there, just stood there, suddenly disenfranchised, suddenly purposeless.

You sent me out into the night. I left my apartment without you to walk the streets. Your silence roused me into action. We couldn't bear to be together at that moment. The roads were littered with strings of ripped red ribbon and plastic, soft fragments of burst balloons. They clung to the sidewalks and streetlights like used condoms. It had rained and little puddles reflected the night-lights. I walked on, into noise and traffic of night revellers. Steam hissed through air vents. In strange formations people walked past me. You never knew the danger I was in because of you, in your desire for serenity you never felt my skin prickle, my heart fluctuate wildly, never saw adrenaline push itself into a redness to my fingertips. The night clothed itself about me. I'd never seen the sky so black, and so fragrant with dangerous proximity. I felt it would close upon me and I would never escape. Claustrophobic stars painted on the inside of a balloon.

Stars and knives and jeers and singular terrors. Eyes like pulsating machine lights. Tears of passing strangers, threats from passing hooligans too fear-ridden to see they were buffoons, just like the rest of us. Strangers jostling for territory and self-esteem. The knife was their crutch, their ego-boosting trip to manhood. I decided to tell you nothing about them, the way they touched me, mocked, made me fear sounds, grabbing at me round corners and alleyways full of boots and black jeans. I scurried past, a mouse in a black coat. There were many shades of black out there in the darkness. Black on the walls, grey the pavement, darker black the road surface, the sky pulsating blue-black. The deep black of my polished shoes. My shadow vanishing into shadow. And in the distance the pulsating glow of a single blue light bulb.

3

I fetched you hotdogs from a stand sheltered under the canopy of a department store. As I waited for the sausages to sizzle and steam, their fleshy skin ripping and bubbling in the heat, I watched the ribbon-like shop window lights changing and racing round the edges of the pane. Red chased blue and then green, re-starting with blue and catching up with red again. I walked to your apartment where I sat on dingy steps full of pink grit with another women who had a rip in her stockings from her knee to her toe. I kept wanting to tell her. The rip fascinated me: her flesh so white against the dark of the stockings. She looked up to your floor or your window. She stood stomping her feet as if cold. I just sat, eating your hotdog, and watched her fidget. She had dark hair, like a silted river. I was exposed in that night air and you never knew. What were you doing still at my house, and why weren't you here? Did you need me to experience the shades of black for a reason? Black of depression, black of uncertainty, black of the woman's stockings, the black-brown of river mud.

It was 4am when I returned to my apartment block. Nothing had washed away the remnants of balloon. They lay over the buildings and roads like casualties, painting the walls a fading blue and red. The basket had gone, as had the bodies. I climbed the stairs. You never knew how close I was to returning to you just as I had left, even though it was you who had sent me away.

There was a man coming towards me. I guessed you had never seen him. He spoke to me. He said, "It's cold here. You shouldn't be about." His accent wasn't native. I liked his concern. I liked that he cared even though I'd only ever seen him between these walls, the lights and the shadows outside. That he was unformed in sunlight. I thanked him and watched myself taking the careful boat home, back across the oceans with him, tasting every salty sea-mile in my throat, watching every spurned wave vanish, return to where I had left. But I didn't; I said thank you, bashfully and entered my apartment. But he had shown me possibilities.

You hadn't moved. You sat catatonically on the leather sofa. The leather looked lighter under the angled lamps. The lighted circles creating patches of white in the black. More shades of black. The sofa was black but here was white?

You said, "The balloon felt like skin. I reached out to touch it. It almost burnt me. Did you see it falling? The fabric crashing? My mouth was open and all my love flew out." Then you fell silent again. It was the last thing you said to me. You slept. I pushed you back against the sofa, tucked your knees under your chin and sat on my haunches to watch you.

Tears in my lava lamp coalesced, and unravelled almost as soon as they had joined, drifting apart. Bits of orange inside the glass bottle split into two, then crashed against the sides and began reforming into tear shapes once more. The dawn seemed late that morning as I sat there watching you, waiting for shadows to lift from the brick walls. Later I moved over to the window and watched the salvage men taking away the scraps of balloon that had so deflated your mind. As I watched you breathing, I thought about crossing oceans for love, about new frontiers, of moving away from here and deeper into the continent.

I said to you, "I never go back." Dawn was here. People shifted out of sleep. Coffee cups all over the city collided with Formica in morning rituals. The apartment felt energised in the low hum of morning. I said it again, "I never go back." I walked to where you lay like a child. "I never go back." I whispered it into your ear. Your hand flickered, as if a fly had bothered your dreams.

When people change and dreams fade and vanish into walls like last season's wallpaper, we should move on. I'd see my friends clinging to the past as if it was the only reality they could recognize, as if reality never changed.

You had walked in here a different person. You made me leave like someone new. That morning when you woke up, looked at me, rubbed your eyeballs, your face pale and tumultuous like waves, and rested your elbows on your knees, I knew I couldn't stay with you, with your lovelessness. I didn't know what you wanted me to do now. What use could I be to you? Soon afterwards, abruptly and silent, you stood up, walked away, catching my lava lamp with the side of your leg. As it fell the orange insides flowed to the opposite end.

From my window I watched you walk down the street. I watched you watching the workmen. A truck followed closely behind you, crunching over broken glass. You paused, letting the truck pass and then you bent to pick up a scrap of balloon, which you tucked in your pocket before mingling into the morning collision of traffic and bodies.

Ramblista

The tape begins: *We were born within two months of each other. Our mothers were sisters from a good family in Scotland. They liked to do things together, always together. Why do you think we are like this?*

I am putting away my notebook, letting the two women giggle, and I turn off the tape machine.

"Thank you Madame Armand. Thank you, Signora. Same time tomorrow?"

"Where are you going? We haven't finished yet!"

"We've only just started. Resume recording."

Tape: *It was typical of our mothers to have their children two months apart. They'd always been extremely competitive. My mother fell pregnant almost within moments of her sister's miscarriage.*

Kristi: "If she hadn't I would have been the elder."

We were born in the autumn. I am a September child; she is November.

And I loved her from the beginning.

Kristi: "That's sweet."

Rosella: "It is, isn't it, but don't go writing that down."

The cousins live in Barcelona, in separate but abutting houses between the Rambla and the Barri Gotic. I asked them why they lived in a less than salubrious part of town and not further out in the better areas. They said they preferred to be where the life was.

They are very wealthy, but not old; and yet something about them reminds me of things past, though they are only in their late fifties. Still young. They sit on their roof terrace, amidst the scramble of other buildings, in the sun with their drinks and their friends while acting as if they're waiting for something, watching the sky darkening, watching the hills of Montjuic and Tibidabo change colour. Sometimes I join them, drink in hand, and I too watch the sky darken. We chat to the always-changing occupants of the adjoining roof, as they water the geraniums, or while they're sunbathing, desperately catching the last dribble of light. The cousins love their open rooftop, shared by both their houses, despite the lack of sea view. These rooftops display more life than the sea, they say. They are fun, these cousins. Once both were exquisite beauties; I wouldn't be here if they were good old Plain Janes.

I am Mathew French, a researcher attached to an agency in London. I find facts. I travel the world checking facts for people and currently my task is the cousins' story. The cousins are so similar; it is difficult to tell their voices apart. It is almost as if they have merged into one. They dress slightly differently: Rosella has beautiful legs and likes to show them off with split skirts, while Kristi has thick ankles, which I glimpse occasionally beneath her palazzo pants.

A client has sent me here. I don't know who, or why. I am just told where to go and what to find out.

I turn on my machine, replay the tape, and listen to their wonderfully clear voices.

Tape: *What she did I would have to do too. At first, this started in a small way. She went horse riding; I went horse riding. She wanted a puppy; I wanted a puppy. When people bought us gifts for Christmas they had to be variants of the same thing otherwise we would have coveted each other's and presumed the other had received the better gift. Once my doll lost its eye and so I made Kristi poke one out of hers, from which I got immense satisfaction.*

And I was inconsolable. My doll looked maimed.

But you did it. You made her one-eyed and we were the same again.

We were like copies of our mothers, and like sisters in all but relationship. We followed each other to university; Rosella did Drama and English, I the new Psychology. When Rosella dropped out, so did I, even though I was enjoying my course and had plans for an academic career.

Kristi followed me to Europe. We wandered around, hitting one place after another. We were young, free and beautiful. On hot beaches, she'd pick up my dumped boyfriends, only to throw them away again and we would giggle at these hapless fellows who enjoyed bedding us both. We kept notes. Mental notes. We could tell you how a certain young man in Montpellier liked to fuck at a window just above his father's head, as if he was fucking his parents and loving it.

"As fascinating as this is," I cough, "What has it to do with my brief?"

The cousins are in good form today. It is almost as if they have sat up all night talking to make sure they get it just right, or to make sure that they don't forget anyone. They sit there, wearing shades, drinking champagne, immaculately dressed and looking beautiful for all their age. Bone structure, sucked in cheeks, smooth brows, crow's feet and sheer shiny lipstick. Their voices deep and striking, and similar in sound. Their candour surprises me; I must be ignorant of the freedom money brings.

"Everything is to do with your brief. If you don't know all the facts, how can you choose which ones are relevant? Turn on that tape-recorder."

I wander the Ramblas, through the Boqueria where the smell of fruit is intoxicating, down to the Placa Reial where I sit with the other snoozers in the afternoon sunlight and just watch people walking by. A man sits next to me wearing a rough woollen jacket and smelling of beer. He folds his arms, closes his eyes and immediately begins snoring. Everything is both frenetic and relaxing, while the sun wilts me like an unwatered flower. So much life is here. Sometimes I think I catch sight of the cousins, dancing on delicate feet in and out of shops, smiling, smiling. I can believe that everyone in the world will walk past me promenading in the afternoon sun.

Tape: *I became a model. So clichéd. But that's what a girl had to do. The family was horrified. Nothing flash, nothing important. Soap adverts, tights. Very few became stars in those days.*

Rosella: "There was the Shrimp."

Kristi: "I know there was The Shrimp. I was there."

Meanwhile Rosella was in Argentina. On horseback. A different kind of whoring. A very different kind of looking good. She hated it when I got a career, such as it was, so she went out to Argentina and began breeding horses, and married a beautiful man who died suddenly.

Rosella: "Mathew, I have to say, you do not look good today. You are too pale and too thin. You need us to look after you while you're here. We hate to see a man not enjoying himself."

Rosella, the eldest, comes towards me, walking loosely, languidly. She is tall, eyes like lemurs', immaculately made-up, and conscious of her every movement, constantly assessing how she will be regarded. Her voice easily slips into French, and I can't follow. German and Italian are my second and third languages. Her accent is superb. Her cousin laughs and looks out of the window.

They have no idea why I am here and don't care. I think they love having someone interested in their lives. I could have been a burglar, a con man.

Tape: *Sometimes our rivalry took on a dangerous edge. Kristi went parachuting in a publicity bid to become an actress after I accompanied Jacques on an archaeological dig on the Peloponnese, near 'sandy Pylos', where we discovered some beautiful coins and statuettes in gold.*

"You were an archaeologist?" I ask, surprised. An intellectual side to her I had never imagined.

Tape: *God forbid, no. I was sleeping with Jacques. When the press got hold of it, it was me they featured and she hated it.*

Kristi: "Don't forget I nearly died."

Rosella looks at her strangely. "Oh yes," she says. "She nearly died."

Tape: *I fell to the ground so hard. Broke my back. It's still fragile. I received wonderful publicity. And she hated it!*

That night they invite me for dinner, at Kristi's house. I expect more anecdotes about their mischievous past but nothing comes. We talk about Barcelona, the Spanish, the Sagrada Família, and I keep expecting them to tell me they'd known Gaudí, Picasso, Joan Miró, or at the least Dalí, but they never mention them. Kristi's house is full of the overpowering smell of fresh freesias. I wander through, looking at her fabulous things, her Fabergé eggs, paintings and jewellery, while she smiles as she watches.

"It's almost a copy of Rosella's," I say to her.

"Do you think so? Is there no difference? No differences between us at all?"

We eat *arroz con langostinas*, followed by sickly sweet crêpes in an orange sauce: neither too heavy, too fancy nor too plain. Then we drink a classy sherry, sweet on the lips, and argue about the need for diverse experiences, the need to experience as much of life as possible – for which you need money – before death; they say, "Don't you think so, Mathew? Have you experienced different sorts of things yourself? You must see fascinating places."

I say, "I am always working."

"And you don't wish it were otherwise?" Krista looks at me and for a second I see the passionate, exciting woman she must have been. I am almost dazzled.

"I believe you can get as much from life if you're poor, from a small canvas, as a large one. A view can be just as valuable and as pleasurable as diamonds. And sentiment is even more important than just money to go sailing around the world or something."

Rosella asks if I really believe this. I nod. Rosella leans forward, and says; "I could describe to you…"

Kristi taps Rosella on the fingers and whispers, "Don't, Ros, leave him be." Then she smiles and they continue eating.

Night falls. I excuse myself and hurry to my hotel. Glad to be alone.

I look out of the balcony at the city in motion: scooters, couples walking casually from one bar to another across the street, the sound of people coming home, or just going out. My room can't compete with Barcelona on a summer's night so I go out to join the noise.

Tourists are on their way up to Montjuic where the Olympics had been held and where each Friday night they stage a dreadful display of water fountains dancing in time to classical music. I decide to go there instead of some bar at the end of the Ramblas.

It's in full swing by the time I arrive. People everywhere, exotic in bright colours and strange accents. I stumble up the steps to the main fountain, which flies upwards and outwards, spurting its water like a displaying peacock, but in varying pastel shades of orange and yellow. I get covered. But it is the music that does me in: vulgar Tchaikovsky, exuberant Rimsky-Korsakov in gaudy syncopation with the pastel lights, the spurting water. The sound of people oohing at the lights.

I look beyond the water, into the distance and on the perimeter of the fountains stand many groups of barcelonès, some looking towards the fountains as if not really seeing anything there at all, others looking down at their shoes. They are mainly men. I walk towards them, and watch as they drift away as if released, and unravelling like a thread. Their shoes click on the marble steps.

The music is loud, the fountains crass, the tourists glib. I look for authentic experience. Some men walk quietly, stopping to mumble to companions and to others going up the steps, before heading down to waiting cars. Others go further into the dark, where, by the trees, two men and one woman are fucking. I stand protected by a tree, and watch. They aren't completely naked, though I can see the woman's brown legs and brown nipples; she is lying on her back, the two men over her. One is fucking her, his trousers halfway down, the other is licking her nipples. Her eyes are closed and she grimaces in pain. One man comes and the other takes over.

From the side I hear a noise, but I am too engrossed in what I see to listen. I've never seen anything like this before, live pornography; and I wonder if the act itself is pornography or the fact that I am watching, which makes it so?

A man appears from the dark and stands beside me, spouting loud Spanish, which I can't catch. The threesome continues undisturbed. The man pulls me by the collar away from the tree. I shout. Another man grabs my balls and squeezes hard. The pain is excruciating; I can't even whimper.

The fountains dance to Beethoven's Fifth, and the air fills with water.

I am crying as they pull me away from the pornography, and down to a dirty corner full of condoms, matches, and sweet wrappers, where they push my head down to the floor. I swallow gravel and spit out cigarette butts. A foot is on my back. I pass out.

*

"Aren't you even curious why I've been sent here?"

"Oh no," Kristi says. "We always knew someone, one day, would want to know."

"Want to know what?"

"Everything we do."

Tape: *Later in life, we stop doing daredevil things. Become quite establishment. Kristi even runs out with a few lords and such, plays with the hunting set, and I marry an old French banker from Nice. These people really think they're so wonderful because they were born with money. The born rich have such appalling manners.*

"That's not fair. Some of them can be quite charming."

The cousins look at each other and smirk like a couple of schoolgirls. At the same time they both say: "Tony Johannssen! The computer king."

"And he made millions with ice-cream. Delicious ice-cream."

The two women are like coquettes from another era, eyelashes flickering, thighs wriggling, and eyes squinting.

Tape: *Rosella got Tony J to cover her in ice cream and he licked it all off, of course.*

It was bloody freezing, but worth it.

They had strangely ignored my black eyes, and my multi-coloured jaw, and had decided to play silly girls. I let them. The tape whirrs.

The day is so bright I am wearing shades inside, and Kristi's house smells of freesias and cherry lemonade. I wonder if they'd run with the rock and roll crowd in the Sixties.

"Well, not really. Rosella once had a fling with some bass player but refuses to tell with which band."

"I haven't finished talking about Tony J."

Tape: *Because Kristi had Tony J, I had to get one of my own.*
   Even though she was married.
   I mean, being covered in ice cream isn't that risqué.
   Back then it felt a little mischievous but not sophisticated. So, I wanted to go one better.
   You always did. You never ever let me have the last word.

I stay in my hotel room that night, and lie in the bath listening to the phone ring and listening for the street sounds. I lie for hours in my bath wrinkling; I have a pale body, thin and bookish in attitude. Sometimes I wish I were strong, like real men: with black moustaches and sweaty hands and deep grunts.

I find the cousins sitting on the rooftop the next day. Sometimes I think, looking at the hills, the messy plethora of satellite dishes on the walls around me, that I will never again return home to Reigate, which to me is like an alien place compared to here; and Grace, my wife, is just a shadow on the lawn.

Tape: *There was a time when Rosella used to spy on my house to find out what I was wearing to some do, or she used to bribe Bonnie to tell her where my clothes came from.*
   Do you remember that time we arrived in the same pearl outfit because you wouldn't tell me what you were going to wear?
   And then you used to visit Madame Marie in Le Salon to get her to put aside the best outfits for yourself.
   You would have done it too.
   Perhaps, but the point is I didn't.

Our clothes were quite the thing. Once we went to a party in Spetses where our clothes were the talk of the night. Such a party. No one holds them like that anymore. People had come from all over the globe.
   Was that the night we made Kerenza Williams take off that vile cerise dress and wear one of ours? And she started crying? Can you believe it? An old-style society gal like that in such floods of tears. And then you beat her later in a swimming race. After I dropped out.
   She was determined to beat you. But she didn't and neither could you beat me, even though you're younger!

And her boyfriend we saw in the library comforting her. She was a pathetic mess, crying. I saw him pull her skirt to one side and touch her between the legs and she loved it.

And then later she said that her boyfriend wasn't there at all. And we thought it strange because we'd seen him in the library in full view. And I think he saw us too. I remember those eyes. Nordic; could even have been a brother to Tony J. Only Tony J hasn't a mean bone in his body.

That guy did.

Rosella, you've been watching too many Hollywood movies.

He did. He was cold. We never did discover who he really was. Kerenza was always getting herself fixed up with businessmen, or married men. A married businessman, that's all we knew.

But why did she say he wasn't there?

Strange business.

People do odd things all the time.

Like the time you got into Reiki healing because I was wearing crystals.

"And now?" I ask, conscious perhaps we were coming to the end of the narrative. Though I knew they didn't want me to go.

Tape: *Now we live quietly. We've seen princes with their pants down, been expensive whores in our youth – not real whores, but you understand what I mean?*

Tape: *We've seen things, done things, and now...*

There was nothing left for them to do. They would become old, eccentric women, whom people would laugh at as their wrinkles deepened, their make-up glistened falsely, as their clothes cheapened and aged them, as the hair-dye bill lengthened. Once beautiful, up to date, and as fresh as butterflies, soon they would be ragged, tawdry like old toys. They should have died young.

As I leave them smiling, standing there waving back at me, I wonder if the memories were true, and how much of this tape was really true?

I spend my last night wandering the Ramblas, the women in corners, the people chatting in the cafes and bars: busy, vivacious and vibrant. In

15

Reigate, all we hear are the shouts of the teenagers on their way to London and the constant drone of traffic.

Tomorrow, after landing at Gatwick, and driving to my semi-detached cottage down a Reigate back street, I shall walk in on Grace crying in the kitchen. And I will stumble upstairs to unpack, and as I retrieve my guidebooks and my sun-stained clothing, I will pull back a fabric blind that feels like parchment, to look across the narrow street and see houses very much like mine and know I shall probably be here the rest of my life.

The tape will be handed in, with my notes, all the facts checked, and the person who requested the material will use what I found or not. I will move on to the next job.

Eighteen months later, after many other trips to Europe, I receive a newspaper clipping and a letter. I open the letter, absent-mindedly, drinking coffee, looking down the long thin untended garden of lawn and a few rowdy trees. It's official. Big fancy headed notepaper. I wonder what on earth I have done.

I read the clipping first, a black-and-white photo of Rosella and Kristi, taken at some regatta in France. They are holding up a cup. Someone is spraying champagne like it is the Monte Carlo Grand Prix. I smile wryly and wonder what trouble they've got into this time.

The previous year, a biography of society hostess turned charity queen Kerenza Williams had been published which had included something about the two, and I had recognized my material there. It must have been her biographer who hired my agency.

The headline: *The fabulous cousins found shot dead.* At first, I think I've read the wrong headline for the wrong picture. I continue reading: *Robbery was the motive, it says. It is suspected they entered from an adjoining rooftop while the maid was off duty for the night. The police are requesting her to come forward as she has not been seen since the two women were shot. She is not suspected at this time, but the police think she will be able to help them with some questions.*

I read it again, and keep staring at the two smiling faces. Then I recall the lawyer's note, which informs me that the two cousins had left me any item of my choosing from either of the two houses. I am to arrange with Hedder, Jenkins and Jackson to choose something from the houses at my convenience. A personal message from the two women would be given to me once I had picked my gift.

I show it to Grace,

"Were they rich?"

"Grace!"

"I didn't know them, why should I care? Are – were – these women rich?"

"I guess so. Jewellery, antiques, that sort of thing."

"I bet you wouldn't know."

"I am a researcher."

"Sometimes, Mathew, you wouldn't be able to research your own name, unless it was sewn inside your socks."

I go straight from the airport to the houses, and a man in a sports jacket and canary yellow polo shirt waits for me. I can't imagine this guy is from Hedder, Jenkins and Jackson, but he shakes my hand like a Yank, says his name is Beauchamp, junior partner, and then he leads me inside.

"The house is exactly as they left it. You're to have first pick of whatever you want. The letter will explain everything."

"Can't I read the letter first?"

Beauchamp shakes his head. "'Fraid not, condition of the will and all that."

The house smells of them: freesias, cigarettes, Chanel perfume. I am in Rosella's house, though it matters not; they are indistinguishable. I wander round, going up and down the marble stairs, touching this and that object. The Sèvres china, Aubusson carpets, the Louis XIV chairs, the Chinese lamps, the photographs, the clothes. I go to Kristi's house. More freesias, Chanel and lavender polish. Beauchamp follows me silently, as if he's itching to get away to do something more interesting. Should I go for something expensive to sell, to make Grace happy to move from Reigate? Or something to remember the cousins by? Pictures of them? Something more sentimental?

"What's the most expensive thing here?"

Beauchamp comes forward, looks at a list.

"Both Kristi and Rosella collected Fabergé eggs. Kristi's diamonds, Rosella's emeralds. But I'm not allowed to give you exact figures. You're to pick."

Upstairs, I rifle through jewellery; into the living room, and look at the collection of photographs, people they'd known, life they'd led: the vases, the china, the paintings. I want to scream. I don't understand why these women had picked me at all. Okay, let's start out with what I don't want. The furniture, the portraits of either woman, the photos, the carpets, the china.

Something keeps telling me to go for the most expensive. Not the most beautiful, not something I will want to keep. But should I take anything from these women at all? Haven't they heirs?

"What would you take?"

Beauchamp looks flustered and surprised. "I don't know... I..."

"See? It isn't that easy." I look at the view and think I'd like to take that.

Finally, I decide. Beauchamp looks relieved. "Here's the note. You may keep it. Sign this. That's your legal receipt. Now I do have to be off."

And it's done. No turning back. No more prevaricating. The road is dry and dusty. It's lunchtime and it suddenly quietens. Even the seagulls are silent. I'm starving and very light-headed. I open the letter. The envelope is apricot-coloured, thick, and written on in fine spidery writing. Pale blue ink.

"Please take the note to your hotel. And play the tape."

I sit on the balcony. I put the tape in the machine and hesitate before I press 'play'. I don't want to hear their voices again. Someone is shouting in the street in thick Catalan.

Suddenly they're here. Both voices, both women, laughing, filling my dull hotel room with exotic life.

Tape: Kristi: *Mathew, we so liked having you in our home that we thought we'd leave you something in our wills. So in the light of recent events, we hope this is a 'just in case!'*

Do you remember that biography of Kerenza Williams that came out last year that used your interviews with us, and mentioned that incident concerning Kerenza and her mysterious boyfriend? The writer of the biography claims it was a certain brutish businessman, with rather vulgar connections, whose name, even here, we daren't mention. Nothing has been the same since. Our life has changed. We considered leaving, but Rosella refuses to be bullied. This man is renowned for his great sense of privacy. The biographer may even be in danger. We don't think that you are though.

Ever since then we have been harassed, frightened and even threatened in the street. As soon as we read the book and realized it was him whom we saw Kerenza with that night, we knew something would happen. He is not a man who likes his secrets to be revealed. Who is to say what else went on that particular night that we know nothing about? Who knows what else he was involved in that night? Perhaps he wasn't even meant to be in the country. And he may feel we are witnesses to his presence. A threat to him. It cannot be a coincidence. If only we hadn't gone, even if only Rosella hadn't insisted on beating Kerenza in that race, in making her change dresses, in following her to the library, he wouldn't think we know more than we do. We are always trying to outdo everyone else and look what could happen!

Rosella is wearing a siege-mentality face. She hates to be beaten at anything.

Rosella: *But importantly, Mathew, you're our guinea pig! We want to test you. Whatever you have chosen will prove one of us right. In fact, in two ways you will prove one of us right.*

You may go for something expensive, as Kristi suggests; or you may pick something of sentiment, staying with what you believe to be true, in which case I shall have guessed right. I really believe this will happen; you won't fall for monetary value, will you? You seemed so certain, so sneering. And at last I want to be right and I want sentiment to stand against mere possessions.

In picking one of our items you will choose between us and ultimately one of us will have had the last word, even though we won't be around to know. But you will know, Mathew, you will know. What is it to be, Mathew? Who has won?

Back in Reigate, Grace asks what happened, what did I do. I tell her it was a joke. There was nothing. For weeks I wonder what to do. I am torn and mortified by what I chose. I think of Rosella and Kristi and of Reigate and the Ramblas, and then it comes to me. It's very simple.

Then weeks later, while on assignment in Paris, I write a letter to Grace. I tell her I am staying on, I tell her I don't know where I'll be going next. I say move on. I tell her I have left her some money. I do have regrets, but I can't let them or anyone else dictate my life now.

With me, throughout all the places I go, all the sights I see, I keep, tucked inside my guidebooks, like a bookmark, a picture of Kristi's Fabergé egg that I chose. The real thing, of course, is with a true collector.

The Ruins of Lutz

They came down from the mountains to the valley and saw the ruins of Lutz. Once Lutz was the most beautiful spiritual city in the world, with colonnades and columns and statues as exquisite as Rome but without the bureaucratic pettiness. Even Marco Polo had said so. Jonas before he died had said so.

They descended the vertiginous sheep path to the flat coastal plain. Lutz bore no resemblance to the pictures and drawings Fisk had seen. He recognized nothing. Jonas, he thought, is it the right place? Have you brought us to the right place? They walked into the city; straight uneven cobbled thoroughfares led precisely to a flat, spacious plaza. Strange coruscating light struck the base of half-bitten columns forming a semicircle around the market area. Looks like Trajan was here, said Inga, wrapping her arms around the frieze-bearing marble. To the right of the Civil Plaza Inga estimated lay the spiritual side of the city. Straight ahead was the sea, the river estuary. The opposite bank seemed almost touchable and further east lay the sea proper.

They settled down by the water's edge, laying out blankets. No need for tents, said Inga. We'll be safe. Nothing will find us here. Neither of them could believe they were truly in the mythic ruins of Lutz. And without Jonas.

It took some time mapping the place with their equipment, rationalizing the ruins, the living space. Inga became ecstatic the day she found the fabled boundary line between the Spiritual and the Mundane. A small wall, she said, made of the lightest granite studded with amethyst. Someone hammered in amethyst? Fisk said, Is that possible? Come with me, I'll show you.

The wall was submerged in water – she'd only found it by diving. There were amethysts, untouched fresh as dew shining glowing under water. How much of the place is under the water, he said, fresh green warm water rushing up his knees and groin.

At night they sat up under the stars and read to each other from texts that referenced Lutz, or wrote notes in dusty notebooks about their discoveries. Sleeping together with their backs turned. It felt strange to be alone in the vastness of Lutz, like inhabiting a nonsensical dream. Lutz was that, nonsensical. Vanishing and hidden and reappearing in history like a myth.

They'd travelled months to get here. Many hadn't believed that Lutz existed. It was a fable. Fisk had a fascination for hidden places and Inga had made a life study of Lutz. She knew all the references in every book, from Pliny to the monkish Mercator the Elder. She knew all the myths, from the Indian to the Turkish, that discussed Lutz. Lutz inhabited her heart like a lover. Yet their journey didn't begin specifically to find the fabled city. It had evolved into it, especially after they'd met Jonas on a small dusty island in the Mediterranean off the east coast of Greece. Jonas had said he knew it could be found, he seduced them with guarantees and wonders he'd heard about. Life is for grabbing, he said, in a bar overlooking the Peloponnese. Don't wait for second chances that never come. He smiled, languorously, fondling vagrant hair creeping down before his eyes. And looked away back into the town where he seemed to be living, they were never certain, with a young man of eastern European extraction, somewhere from the depths of the Caspian Sea, he would proclaim in a voice redolent of the London stage. Jonas had been sent to them, Inga later said. Fate, she said, fate. She never liked it though when Jonas had taught him to meditate. Do you no good, she'd said and she'd laughed.

Inga warned Fisk of the fable – do not take stones from the City of Lutz for it is said whoever does so will be pursued by the city itself and brought back and stoned. Creepy, said Fisk. What if a stone snucks into your shoe or your pocket from under a fingernail?

The days and nights grew hotter as if the city, the timeline and the sky had shifted into a new season without warning, almost arbitrarily like moving a line across a page. They mapped the streets, measured cobbles, cleaned jungle away from frescoes of demons and elephants and dancers in deferential poses, uncovered stupas in miniature, discovered small places of worship and areas for entertainment, recitals said Inga, like Greece, plays and such. Lutz is older than Athens, she said, far older. There's meaning in these frescoes. A story. A story for us to find. It talks about visions and spectacle and the initiated being granted access to paradise. Can you see this figure here, creeping forward, a small blue figure. He's going forward. This other fresco shows images of destruction, sexual union and the stealing of hearts. Fascinating, she says, brushing dust and grime away from the plaster. Wondrous.

Fisk would stop and look at Inga, who was so energetic covered in freckles and so different from him despite them being twins with her small tough frame, her thin waist, and hair cropped like a man's. He understood looking at her working why they had to come, it was as if her life could not be complete until they had done this, that her flat back in the too familiar city of their home held nothing for her. At night sometimes she would leave where they slept and go to the just uncovered Mound of Meeting and watch over the city like she was its guardian. She was waiting for the city to work itself upon her, for the spiritual to enfold her, for something of significance to happen, for this was the place of closeness. The ruins of Lutz had been with them since childhood and Inga wanted to know every inch of it, every moment of existence in it, sleep was for fools. Fisk worried that her quest for knowledge and discovery was burning her out inside. Sometimes he'd discover her over some plaque of significance, an indication of habitation or spiritual need, dusting a face whose nose and lips were partially disintegrating, bent double over it clutching her belly. She looked up hearing his footsteps, women's thing, she uttered gently, as if forcing the words from distended lips. Then she would stand up and continue though her walk would be a hobble. She paled. It had been Inga who had left Jonas beneath a mango tree on a plateau high in the mountains. They avoided the certain parts of the river for it was populated with crocodiles and hippos. One day Fisk was bitten by a snake and had to lie still for hours while his body filled and swelled with poison and Inga prayed that he wouldn't die. God was merciful.

The sea retreated from the city shape, daily revealing more of what was lost until at length the amethyst wall was exposed to the sunlight. Fisk imagined the stones attracting the light so brilliantly that every thief for miles would see their reflection in the sky and make a grab for them. Then failing would run to the source, running out of the jungle that surrounded Lutz, running down to the plains, and coming for everything that was here.

They had still to find the secret heart of the city which must be buried under the water. After the Mundane – with its areas of commerce carefully laid out in grids – came the Spiritual with its temples and places of peace, with its areas of Devotion, most of which was only now being revealed. Daily they'd stand at yesterday's tide edge and find it retreating, and now there was more to go into, to spread themselves – Inga liked to sleep in different places for a few nights at a time, always moving on, always careful with the fire she lit for food. Every other day she was moving closer and closer to the Centre: the moment of pilgrimage heart. The place, according to ancient sources, to which all Devotees came head bowed, resplendently dressed to do honour to the Temple of Lutz, the spiritual capital of the nation. As people they'd been proud of Lutz and had even tried rebuilding it after the devastating earthquake that had destroyed it so long ago. Inga wanted to reach the Centre – to find the one true Temple of Lutz. Fisk tried to calm her and said it may not exist. She crinkled her nose like a small child at a distasteful smell.

When the bells sounded both were asleep. The middle of the night, only crickets and frogs kept tangible existence alive, and they'd been working till last light. Inga liked to be up before dawn. She said she wished she could meditate like the Divines used to but it was outside of her knowledge. You're burdened by Catholicism, Fisk would say, and she'd turn from him unable to hear such words. Instead, at dusk she would light candles, tiny tea lights bought in Bangkok months and months ago, when they never believed Lutz was real or that if it was it could ever be found, despite what Jonas had said, all over the circular plateau that was once the heart of the recital area, steps now falling to the sea. Or sometimes she'd light them, kicking away fat spiders and tiny reptiles, in the lotus-shaped bath that she'd found around the corner in a wild garden area they assumed was once residential. Huge tumblers of church incense would burn every night and in Latin, head bowed, hands folded like a Buddha's, she would pray, on her knees sometimes. This deeply religious side to his sister he found hard to understand. Spiritual yes – for their quest for the past and particularly the ruins of Lutz, wasn't that spiritual? Everyday he thought that he was performing some god-like mission though who the god was and why he would want this, he left to Inga to fathom.

Then the bells sounded. They woke suddenly, looked at each other and stood up. It's coming from over there! Fisk pointed to a section that comprised almost a whole house partly roofed. On the rare occasions it had rained they had sought shelter there but hadn't explored further. Now they ran. They saw a tower behind the trees. Lutz was really the jungle's home. Palms crawling with the vines lianas, philodendrons, bamboo, orchids on trunks, huge ferns. They were getting closer to the sound of bells. It was almost like an awakening, a calling to the absent faithful to come protect the city, to the hiding militants in the hills, the forgotten in the cities, to the memory genes of those who were here, who called Lutz home. The sound was like a bright spotlight falling on them.

We must stop it, said Inga, running. The sound was a tunnel leading to them, a signpost in sound, a signal across hills, like fires of warning.

They didn't understand how a bell could be ringing. But they ran to the origin of the sound. The path was cleared, someone had been there but they found no bell, no housing for a bell. They found nothing but torn bamboo sticks and frayed fern leaves as if someone or something had been standing there biting, tearing the jungle away from this spot.

Inga said, can the place really be haunted?

You're Catholic – you believe in ghosts?

The people of Lutz weren't Christian.
So it is possible for non-Christians to be ghostly and ring bells?
Jeez, Fisk – how the hell should I know?

They couldn't explain the bells. They said nothing further about it. They tried to sleep though the dawn was incipient.

Fisk considered his sister – he loved her yes, but she was unknowable. They once lived together till her fastidiousness and yes he admitted her obsessive religiosity wore him down. They were orphans, from a small Norwegian-in-origin family. She was all he had left and he had clung to her through almost everything and yes he enjoyed her company – she could be vivacious and erudite but he still couldn't understand her. He comprehended much about her but ultimately she was beyond him.

A restless dawn-filled bell ringing sleep followed. No one came, though they expected them. The bells stayed silent after that. Fisk, she said, coming towards him at day-break, we need to go further.

Fisk imagined Lutz full of people, the streets bustling, the people selling, the machinations of darkness. No doubt if Lutz was full of people, full of bars and junk palaces he would investigate people's lives, slip into the undercurrent of the pulse of the city, searching the cornucopia of life for answers. He felt he could relate to that – to the figs in baskets, hanging cloths of calico and silk and carpets in red, brassware like mirrors on shop walls – far more than he could these ruins. Though he could understand the place's attraction. At night he still disbelieved that they had discovered it but it was Inga's place, Inga's crucible of life, not his.

Soft moonlight rang against the brickwork as they sat around the fire. Inga had lit her tiny stellar candles and circulated them around the circular steps so from a distance it looked like she was bent in the centre of heavens. She hummed, walking back to where Fisk sat and said quietly, There's someone out there. Someone watching from the jungle. They both thought of Jonas.

All Fisk wanted to do was breathe in the night air, relax, sleep. He'd given up reading at night as he wanted to save battery power on his torch. He told stories to himself while his eyes were closed and his ears tuned waiting for ringing bells; he told himself stories, dredging up memories of recent events. A bar in Bangkok where he'd chatted up a guy while Inga was in the restrooms and the guy had bought him a beer – he looked big, well muscled, not truly Inga's type but what did that matter? He talked to him about cricket and rugby and his hometown of Adelaide and time. He said to Inga, as she had returned, Adelaide is ten and half hours ahead. Ten and a half! A half! Inga sat next to the bull from the sun and gradually they blanked Fisk out of the conversation. Fisk had nodded and left thinking how long it had been thus, Inga red-lipped and shiny nosed, fresh, wholesome and as healthy as the sky, coming to his friends, men he gradually got to know just for her benefit. Other men would have taken advantage and lived vicariously through their sister's experiences but Fisk was content just being a cog in her life. This was his life, guiding his sister, finding her men, holding her hand, taking her interests as his own. This was how it was between them. They used to sleep in the same bed once as children and he missed that. The innocence of childhood touch, the security of togetherness. Lying back to back under the Lutz summer-night sky, safe in the knowledge of the other's presence was a reminder of that. He could feel her breathing most nights, her back rising and falling, her mouthing slight prayers in her sleep, the words hissing through drying lips into the night air.

He stood up when she repeated again that they were being watched, and mumbled something like who, what, what you mean? But his mind was still in his stories. Inga had chosen to go to university in Ireland to study archaeology so he had followed. She would have been shocked if he hadn't, and both would have been alone.

In silence they walked to the edge of the water, facing the same direction the bells had come from the other night. I heard something, Inga said, there's someone living on the edge of Lutz – they come into the centre at night. Stealing small things and watching us. I have lain here at night and seen them. He asked if she was sure. She nodded. They came closer tonight and stood over me and touched my hair.

They?

Yes, there's at least two maybe more. They're getting bolder. It's worrying.

Why didn't you say anything before?

Because I wanted them to have free rein to see what they did to find out who they were. They may have been an important sign of something.

If you'd have been aware you'd have scared them off.

Fisk was surfacely silent, looking out. The sounds they made reverberated like thunder. The darkened sky picked up the chung of feet, the length of moving limbs, the hiss-breath of syllables into the air, and carried the sounds, like Saturn's rings, around the ruins of Lutz so that even the bricks and fallen columns and pools of water could feel the vibrations. It's like the area, the buildings, the structures were part of a huge speaker, tweeters, woofers soaking up the sound and throwing them out into a spongy night sky, plastic stars listening in to the motion of life. Fisk stepped forward. Waves on the steps. Water like fingers, creeping round crevices. The darkness shapes moving as the sky lightened to midnight blue. The stealth sound of jungle growing. Inga was still, barely moving, barely breathing, one crash of sea-water and everything would tumble. They could feel the wind pushing against the rocks, the darkness shapes were moving again like shadow burglars. Something cut across the steps. A ponderous shadow, a shadow of gargantuan proportions. Fisk felt spooked, Fisk felt hassled and haunted by the depth of blackness of the shadows against the pulsing midnight sky. He wondered if the shadows and the haunting would vanish when dawn came.

Inga moved forward again. The night sounds, unknowable, terrifying, cut across them like a Bach violin partita – all angles and sharpness of symmetry.

Fisk thought he had learnt all there was to know about Inga. Or the world, or himself. He was a stone cast in concrete; a thickness at the heart of life; an imperishable solidity. He always assumed it would be Inga, with her beliefs and desires, who would have something miraculous happen to her. He decided to meditate just as Jonas had shown him. He closed his eyes. Light shapes vacillated through his head. Inga scoffed, that's a waste of time. It's not true, it's a heretic's contemplation.

Outside his head, in that minute, the sky lightened perceptibly again and a bird came out of the darkness and flitted across the centre of the horizon, black wings clashing against blue paling sky. And vanished. Blackness vanishing. And wings crashed against foliage and brickwork moaned and then there was nothing perceptible in the air. Not even a tendril of breath. He forced his eyes open, immersed as he was in the patterns in his head and the feeling of solidity he felt from meditating. Inga appeared to have vanished. He shouted. He rubbed his eyes but everything apart from his immediate vicinity was in darkness. It was as if he were alone. He called out to her but could hear nothing. Fisk stumbled back to the things huddled in the centre of the circular steps, the spotlighted place of oration, Inga had said. This is where poets declaimed and actors recited plays and wise ones came from the Divine and other cities around to talk about the faith and the life and foretell the ending of Lutz.

They knew?

Oh yes the people didn't believe them but they knew. They were told. This is a great earthquake area. Daily they expected to be vanished.

Or vanquished.

Why did they stay here?

Chancing their arm, she said, laughing.

Fisk stood in the middle of their belongings, the sleeping bags sprawled, the books in piles, the food supplies, mainly tins of chilli beans and bottled water, the collection of ripening mangoes, knowing they were there, able to even pick up a tin and examine it but once he moved anything more than an arm length away it vanished. Something brushed against him, a whisper, a strangled shout in his ear, and pondered the significance of being one and not one at the same time. He reached out his hands, called out Inga's name. He sat on his haunches for a while, his hands held together, looking in the direction of where he saw Inga last hoping she would come closer. He recalled being in towns and cities of the desert with Inga some years before, the white buildings, the houses made of dust, the blue paintwork and the face of the distrusting. He remembered protecting her from the eyes of the curious, he remembered a small but beautiful Arab man coming up to him, eyes always on her, he remembered them vanishing together and Inga's reddened, flustered, sweating face in the morning, and the constant rubbing of wrists. He remembered feeling sidelined and worthless. A similar feeling to now only now he also felt abandoned and suddenly afraid. He wished Jonas was here.

Over the last few weeks they had tried to forget Jonas, deliberately forgotten him, forgotten that it was him that led them here. Jonas: exciting, witty, sensual, passionate and probably dead. Fisk wished he was here now and not lying beneath some overgrown tree, food for god knows what creature that he didn't know the name to but Inga would. He never ceased to be amazed at what Inga knew.

Sometimes he dreamt of Jonas, Jonas and Inga together in their tent laughing and stroking, and enjoyed these dreams and didn't, all at the same time. He wanted Jonas to be alive but feared. He suspected Inga had killed him. She wouldn't let Fisk near Jonas's prone body. He's dying, she said. We must move on.

Once he saw Inga standing by a wall on a backstreet. They were in a small fishing village over looking the Mediterranean. The wind was ferocious and hoarse. It was winter and the sun was as bright as new pennies. She'd sent him out to collect supplies and didn't expect him to be wandering the part of the village she was in, and he was able to watch her without her knowing that he was there. He stood on the corner like a spy and watched her waiting for men to approach her and they did. The young men mainly. The older ones watched from the far side of the street and the women didn't even look at her as they walked up the hill towards the market. Fisk held overripe tomatoes and flatbread and batteries in his bag. Supplies for their journey into the desert. Later Inga returned after he did, saying nothing till she turned, laughing and told him a joke about a nun going into an Irish bar.

She seemed subsumed by a cloud of her own making, like a shield around her, a force field. Some nights her bed was empty. And he'd be shocked, for she preferred him to get men for her.

The light changed. Dawn rose, sounds of geese flying through the site and out. A wail of insects hidden in the ferns. Sounds of anger from the other side of Lutz. He scrabbled about for some dried apricots from a sealed bag, and stuffed them into his mouth; without Inga, the city, once becoming as familiar as his face in the mirror, grew suddenly strange and threatening, as if something could emerge unformed and wondrous from the brickwork. The reeds in the water struggled in the growing day. In the distance he could see another stupa, light catching white, wind moving the trees of the jungle. Could it be? The wind was growing. Trees beginning to bend side to side like mad exercisers in a gym.

Inga said Lutz had once covered thousands of acres, maybe even ten thousand acres if you count the manufactured reservoirs. The gardens, the overflowing canals of pumped water, were famous. She would quote Pliny to him, where 'The much loved bejewelled citadel of Lutz,' had been mentioned, she said. Citadel? The Divine would have been behind a citadel? Does spirituality have to be protected from the masses, he asked. Of course, she said. But really I think they were more afraid of what was possible to let out.

The wind gathered and groaned. He moved carefully, tracing the dilapidated walls of the Divine, walking round them, imagining the princess in a story of Lutz who ran away to join a caravan of traders only to be attacked by a pride of lions. The king lion fell in love with her and twins were born – a boy and a girl of their bestial union. Fisk thought the story very strange for a religious text – a bestial union, a woman mating with a lion! This was not what he expected from Lutz. And he wondered what basis in fact it had.

He ate meagrely, chewing mangoes slowly, juice dripping down his chin, and it grew dark. He was too afraid to go anywhere now. He lit a fire and kept to it, huddling his legs, trying not to think of Inga, his twin and yet only being able to think of her. He read more of the Chronicles, some Pliny. At night it would come, he knew it. The night noise grew. The cacophony of sound. The wall-sound of night. He was like this alone and not alone till night fall. It was as if the city was waiting, testing, waiting for the optimal moment. Sometimes he thought he heard noises, felt himself being prodded, a ghostly hand coming out of the fog to shake him out of his reverie, for reverie this must be. A dream. Soon Inga would wake him with tea. He began meditating again.

There's no clouds and the stars were like bright bulbs in the sky. Though it was dark the fire flames reflected the sitting Buddha behind who took on a rather glouring dimension

There's stillness and there's rain. He lifted up his head. Everything's quiet. The silence crowded him. He could feel every piece of existence here, every slow wave to the shore falling over hidden bits of Lutz, every slight breath of wind through the temple remains, over the faces of the Buddhas, over their taut fingers pointing to the sky; he tried to stop hearing his breath, tried then to slow his breathing. Trees squealing like cats, waves as thunderous as engines, Buddhas smiling. He sat very still, almost trying to fit into the background. His head felt empty and dizzy. He wouldn't scream with the loneliness of his fog-like world, nor panic at what he couldn't control. Eyes closed now, wind wrapping itself around him like a chiffon scarf. Leaves fell on him, thin, wispy, crackling leaves with veins that seemed to palpitate as he looked at them; pulsing veins, glowing red in a world of green. He threw the leaves to the ground. Stood up. In the distance the view had changed, cleared even but it wasn't the view he was used to nor had been expecting. The sky seemed to have tightened around his head, he reached up his hands and touched the clouds. He could feel the clouds between his fingers and caressing his palms!

Then he decided to light the candles, despite the wind. So he stood in the centre of the lotus-shaped steps and lit them, watching the flames play carefully on the ascending steps like cracks of light in the midnight dark.

If he could touch the clouds, what else could he touch? He reached out, closed his eyes and there it was. Lutz as he always wanted it: full of life, the cobbled streets, the traders and merchants, the shopkeepers, the green-robed monks, the day in motion, people playing backgammon in the gutters and table chess in the parks, engineers building canals to the reservoirs, children playing at the sea-edge watched on by fretting nannies dressed in peach.

Patterns of the city repeated over and over – arches in lapis blue, triangles in vibrant green built into doorways and windows, a shape similar to a Star of David – a tricolour of red, yellow and white. And Jonas. Plaques, statues of the famous, Buddhas being moved into place, walls of amethyst glowing. He sees the Mundane inhabitants queuing up on Reverence Day to enter into Devotion, monks smiling, male and female in green with small triangles at the hem of the clothes, hair pulled back, neck encircled by the largest red beads, the size of carpenter bees. Someone motions to him. He moves forward, steps up to the glistening Wall of Devotion. He stops, bows his head, feels engulfed in the woody smell of burning sandalwood, sweet, slightly sickly, overwhelming and giddying and lifts his head into something else, a clearing of mist. He stands at the threshold, feeling on the cusp of something and yet half empty and dizzy with visions and aromas. He feels solid and yet capable of flight. Hard and flimsy. There's something here, there's something he needs to know, to see. He steps forward.

A noise behind, a rustling, a shoving and vanquishment in the trees. He can see Inga standing there, a sudden figure in the dark green overgrowth, her face dirty with thick black smudges like coal-fingers have fondled her. Her clothes snagged, torn on brambles. She screams something but her mouth is moving in slow motion. Can you see, he says, can you see it? It's glorious. She shakes her head, holds out her hands, imploring him to come to her.

In the Devotion Jonas is laughing and calling him. Of course Fisk could just ask Inga what she was doing but the real Lutz is too appealing. He says, I can see the Temple of Lutz, the true heart. I can smell it, I can touch it. It is as real as daylight.

Inga steps forward, I see nothing.

You see nothing?

Yes, where? I want to see. I have to see.

Over there. He points to the bells sounding which now he sees like towers over the centre of the Devotion. The temple is there. People are waiting.

He leaves her. She tries to grab his loose shirt but he's gone. His shirt floats way out behind him, a slither of blue cotton falling to the lighted steps. Inga tries to see where he's going, tries to see what he pointed to but the horizon is dark and full of ruins, and it looks like the horizon is splitting into light and dark. Bells come again and Inga is back and is alone.

Eyes like water, like ice

The man just nodded, coolly, detached. Around him small white-clothed men formed the fires, removing red and yellow flowers for paler, less frivolous ones, lighting more incense, throwing rice and saffron, placing bowls of water around the fire, laying a white sheet over the pyre. Someone began a low hum.

The man in beige closed his eyes to the woman beside him, perhaps his wife. At first she'd laughed, hopefully, at the absurdity of his request, then when it became obvious he was serious she'd stood so still, immovable, feeling her stomach quivering, her shoulders shivering. Now she pleaded with him, on the verge of crying.

The crowd couldn't understand. Those that had grasped what was happening couldn't believe it.

It was a big hall; a thousand people had crossed the country to listen to the talk from a small group of Indian mystics who'd left their homes in still, white mountains to bring a whisper of truth. Words from another, more spiritual continent.

At first, the talk had gone well. The mainly white, middle-class audience listened attentively to the words from the small, tiny men, some of whom looked so frail, so bony they must be on the verge of death, and absorbed them inside their heads, like osmosis, planned what they would say to their friends at the after-talk gathering over a bottle of wine. How they felt uplifted by the words. Walking on air, happy with the world till the next talk, the next mystic. Those tiny men, how their faces were so unlined, so pure, all that yoga and fresh air. Pure living.

They'd laughed when the men made a small joke – bright eyes like water like ice, laugh like a child, cuddly like an animal. And the people of the audience were prepared to return home content, while the Indian mystics headed for another city, another hall.

Throughout the talk, the man in beige had said nothing. He neither laughed with the crowd, nor smiled, nor applauded. He wasn't here to worship. His wife had come along reluctantly. And as the talk progressed the reluctance and disbelief faded. He saw worship in her eyes.

The Indian mystics had noticed him. Not at the front of the crowd but within seeing distance. An expressionless face. A static body. He stared at them as if testing their existence. They knew he would ask for something from them.

There was always someone like him. Not always at the front, not obvious and showy, but in the wrong place nevertheless, seeking them out but never coming closer, never touching like other members of the crowd surrounding them with desire and hope.

The fire was higher now. Just little flames eating into the wood, like rapacious insects.

The crying woman feared going near her husband or the Indian men, busy with the preparations, feeding the fires. Chanting. The man in beige stood up now. Not watching the flames but the little men, haunched over, throwing yellow petals. To him they were like little dwarves. Snow White. Happy at work. No one smiled. Or cried. They were as expressionless as him. One's dhoti slipped down his shoulder. He looked up as he pulled it back into place and caught the man's eyes. A flicker of understanding.

Most of the crowd hadn't gone. The fire grew. They wondered how it was contained. Some at the front had moved away from the man in beige, from the fire, and huddled in groups whispering, pointing at the man. Some laughed. Some looked to the open doors for a figure of authority.

The room was getting hotter. More people moved from the centre outwards. The sound of reluctant dying wood filled the auditorium, drowning out the chanting men.

No one approached the man in beige.

He watched the men; they moved around him as if he wasn't there, as if he was a pillar, or a piece of furniture, carefully avoiding any physical contact. They were nearly ready.

Never before had they been asked to do this; and they never considered they would be asked; especially not in the spiritually bankrupt West that no amount of visits by mystics could alter. Perhaps in Northern India: some religious fanatic, a martyr, his own religious quest. But this man had not the look of a fanatic. Tall and well-dressed. Innocuous. So western. He'd spoke gently, firmly. No amount of persuasion could change him. They wondered if he'd been brooding on this matter for some time.

When he'd responded to their question of 'Is there a special spiritual function we could fulfil while in your country?' he'd stood up before any one else could ask anything. Said what he had to say and sat back. The men glanced quickly to each other, waiting for a dissenting voice, the voice of reason and moral value. Normally one amongst them, their eldest, could be relied upon to say what they were all scared of saying. He looked at the man, peering closely, whispered 'Are you sure?' The man in beige nodded. 'I have to.' And the elder leant back, nodding to his companions. 'I give permission for the lighting of the fire.'

The fire was ready. It could not be put out, not at this moment. It could only die back of its own accord. One of the Indians stood up. 'Those who'd like to leave, please do so now.' Then he nodded for the doors to be locked after the crowd had left. Only a fraction of the original crowd remained.

The eldest nodded to the man in beige to come forward. He hesitated. And for the first time glanced at the flames. But he stepped closer, not looking at his wife, ignoring the calls of the crowd behind him.

He touched the hand of the mystic and said some incomprehensible words into his face. Slowly they undressed him, like servants, handmaidens. Gradually each layer of clothing was folded and lay on the floor before him. He stood naked. Then they washed him, slowly, with warmed, light-catching tap water from their dressing rooms. The man stared frontward as they touched him, cleansed his flesh and wrapped white cloth around his body.

They showed him the fire. And stood to one side.

As the man lay on the pyre, crossing his arms, his wife numb now, dried her eyes.

Islands of the Blessed

On the islands of the blessed we like to sing. In the islands of the blessed
we sit and count the grasses we cut, the birds we pluck. In the islands of
the blessed we watch the shadows circle our feet.
They say it is a place of aspiration.

He calls out and I stand up as sudden as a spooked ibis. The cranes call.
A cormorant flock hurries to trees. In the islands of the blessed the man
is home.
 The house made of rushes, the flapping of multi-coloured linen, we
are not as substantial as mud brick. The river is everything.

In the islands of the blessed he makes happiness with his simplicity.
 In the island of the blessed he makes pain with his complications.

Come, he calls, come, they are bombing the cities! We crowd like
beetles around the TV set. Plasma, he says, plasma TV from the city.
 The blankets flap; the wind has risen. I must tie down our exits.

In the islands of the blessed a cruise boat is passing. Night quickens.
Someone is crying, screaming. Today the feluccas are silent but at night
I hear their stealth.

When the sun is at its most brutal – the unrelenting force of a brutal god
– I walk one thousand paces, crossing coast to coast. On the only hillock

– a hummock of houses of ants – I stand, and my elevation is stupendous. In the world of aspiration we are in heaven. So they say. We are the privileged of simplicity. We have the self-sufficiency of survival.

Bathing in the river, hidden amongst the pampas grasses, circled by river cranes, the egret shiver-cries, as sudden as darkness.

In the morning, after the man has gone, I walk from the house, carrying with me bottled water he brought back from the city, jingling with the weight of gold bangles around my wrists, the light touch of a crimson lotus silk scarf on my shoulder, to the other side of the island, near to where the Grump lives, where the tiny river bears play if you're lucky. I want to see if the island has spread its edges, or pulled them in, shrunk, slipped into the river, if a wave from a passing boat tickled the land's edges and blurred them. I tinkle as I move. He buys me too much gold. He buys me things of adornment, not nourishment. He says women should be the public face of his pride. We are to shine and dazzle even in darkness. It is a wonder pilots of the big boats aren't blinded by the women's finery. Our finery, my finery. When he places another bangle on my wrist he looks directly at my eyes, at my irises, at the contraction of pupils and the swimming liquid of the whiteness. He clasps my wrists, pushes back my other gold bangles, pushes the new bangle, shiny, mesmerizing, onto my wrist and mutters some words, incantations, under his breath. Once a year he buys me a new gold adornment. Once a year he reaffirms his possession.

A football match in progress at the far end of the island. Perhaps my daily walks should be lengthways instead of traversing the heart of the flatness. I know I will never truly go anywhere else.

In the islands of the blessed we are lucky with heat, rarely feeling the judgement of rain; we have space, we have solitude and he has visits, processions to the distant city.

Other islands have plant life, collections of trees taller than anything seen along the banks. Other islands are for crops, or for living, here we grow and live in the same space. Sometimes I see people, bedraggled, exhausted, starved after clambering out of the river and now just sitting there on the bank waiting for someone to throw them back. On the island of the blessed there is not room for all.

Every night he expects me beside him, like something that's part of him, an extra finger, another faithful loving arm without which sleep would be impossible. I lie beside him, sounds of egrets and snoring, imprisoned by his expectations, when really I want to be sitting on the river bank, looking across the islands, hidden from the slumbering night boats in the reeds, feeling the night breeze on my face. When we were first together and occasionally I would get up in the night after we had made love, or say I'd be in bed later, he would cuss me, shake his big bear head, a beard so monstrous as to defy belief, he would look at me and at first he'd refuse, forbid, demand my obedience. Then he'd plead and that would win. How could I refuse? Those eyes, that need. I am bound. His very insistence is his vulnerability.

On the islands of the blessed, we can do as we please.

On the islands of the blessed bound by water, waiting for the affirmation of children, in the distance, mountains as jagged as wrenched fingernails. Crossing the island end to end, circling its edges, the crumbling banks, the soft slivers of beaches; walking the island back to the other side, feeling edges, boundaries, borders all around me, watching moorhens slip into the reeds and away, the grey herons screaming as they rise into the air. The barrier of water. The barrier of duty. I search the island looking for the fragrant simplicity of the white jasmine. The images on the obelisk are obscured by the leavings of ibis. We are envied.

Here we sing. Sometimes I think my voice is unbound to me and I am merely its holder, its captive. I am the housing. When I open my mouth the notes escape into the air. They meet the air, they wander, they float. Once realized, they are free. My voice births notes. The birthing pleases him who values fecundity in everything, and he stops to watch me and he smiles. Through his beard he smiles. My singing soothes him and his smile is like a drug.

You look like a witch, with your mouth open, catch flies, catch flies. The Grump is standing before me when I sing, and he looks like a belligerent hover wasp. Once he was a good man and so I am nice to him. Once in the past he taught me how to tame reeds into shape, how to fold them to my doing and how to make sounds that make the ibis silent listeners. I have seen him, on the edge of the island, where the land tapers out to reach the centre of the river, playing into the water, moorhens scattering into places of safety, the black and white kingfishers diving from calcified branches. What is he doing, I think, what can he be doing? He looks like he is charming the fish from the water. Real fishermen pass in their blue boats with their vast nets and jeer at him. This is the island of the blessed.

Why did you encourage me in voice if all you will do is laugh at what I look like?

I hear you've been added to, he says. I look down to my bangles and know he is laughing again. You women, he says, shaking his head. When you were a child I thought you would be different. When I found you hiding in the midnight light when all around you your family and friends slept, when you were supposed to be sleeping still and contained, and I showed you the river at night, I showed you what is here, how to find hidden midnight butterflies, and the flowing Lotus, and let you watch the river bears dancing. I showed you the security of independence. I thought you would find clarity of solitude.

You didn't finish, I say, you left me wondering about more. I know there's more.

He walks away. Is there any point? You let them bind you, Kea, he says, why should I make it worse for you when you do nothing for yourself?

You made me sing! You gave me voice.

He stops, looks at me, and smiles. For a moment I watch his form, deceptively strong, the wind tickles his clothing.

He gave me freedom in song. He gave me dreams in the sky's boundlessness. I sing when alone, I am voiceless in company. I walk back to the house. The wind flapping the cloths, the sticky smell of sandalwood seeping from rush fibres.

Most days I want to travel across the river to the other bank. As a child, bootless, bangleless, I would explore the extreme edges of my island. I would take some thick, filling bread, full of almonds and raisins, softened by olive oil, always freshly made – my mother like all women were in competition about who made the best loaves. To me there was no question. So armed with life-giving bread I would vanish to the covering of the palm trees and sit beneath the dates. The island is full of water, little swirling or stagnant pools, slits where the river cuts into the land, the island is full of sand, and grit and granite boulders which the cranes watch from. As a child I saw a falcon drop from the sky into a slit of penetrating river water and emerge with a tiny fish. He sat on a boulder and tore the fish inside out. I watched him standing there motionless except for his turning, alert head. A falcon of wisdom. The old Grump said the falcon had come to watch over me. This was hard to understand now in the world of bombings on plasma TV screens.

When he wants to watch that screen I have to also. I wish I could turn my hearing off. Some develop this. The men develop this when I speak. When he sleeps I want to dance, when he watches I want to speak, when he goes for long journeys I want to make love. He has the body built for caressing. My mother says, she pounds the flour, when you enter into a relationship you become one and you have to sacrifice individual desires.

I see that he sacrifices much when he goes alone to the city. Is it so wrong to want to stay up late while he sleeps? Or to wander outside while he watches the plasma screen or talks to his friends? Is it so wrong to be alone in the dark sometimes?

Today I am on the opposite river bank, looking back to the island, seeing how small it looks with just a few trees, the ruptured obelisk half-formed, half-eaten at the right side, the brightly-coloured rush houses, the children running round free, the women covered sitting round their houses, hands hennaed, arms smothered in the tingle tangle of gold against gold, and the animals: the goats and cows. The island looks desolate. Low the sun hits it and never leaves, low sun in the morning, high sun till dusk, it moves round the island like a guarding light, a light of torture, we are never free of it. Some places have mountains or caves to hide in. As a child I would hide in the water, amongst the reeds like a moorhen happy alone, and watch my family looking for me. The scintillating water. At certain times the water reclaims the island and we have to leave in our boats. To wait till the river is bored and runs away. We are granted existence between the slits of river.

He is in the city again. I asked to come with him, I said please take me; we could make love in the afternoon heat on fresh white city sheets. He pushed me away and told me not to be so stupid. He did not go to the city for pleasure, for silliness, for decadence.

I have tried to lure him inside the house to make love while the noon day sun burnt a hole in the hanging blanket my mother gave me as a wedding gift but he always shakes me off. I had thought he might be looser in the city, away from the everyday, away from the binds of pride. And the straitjacket of expectations. I had even tried to cajole him, like a little animal, into caressing by the water's edge under the cover of darkness and the revelation of the moon. To join with me in liking the dark, the metallic chill of the night. But he wants none of it; he wants me next to him to confront the loneness of his sleep, comfort, reassure. If I am alone, away from him, this is a threatening thing to him. So I leave the house and cross the island again swift-footing over the hillocks and goat paths. I sit under the banana palms as the sun sets. I should be elsewhere.

In the islands of the blessed we are bound like slaves. Bound by our status, bound by each other's expectations; my mother daily, in silence, pounds rushes. The moorhen wander from bank to bank. I watch the rushes, counting the reeds, the slithers of water opening in the cracks of the ground, wondering if in time these islands will vanish and then where will we aspire to?

One by one a river bear slinks from the undergrowth, small, thin, wiry, more like an upright monkey or lemur than a bear but their bulbous brown nose proclaims their bearness. Four foot high but with strength to tear apart the vagrant cats that linger round human throwaways.

Slowly carefully with precise hesitation, they begin to dance. A leg first, then an arm jostled in motion. Soon they are crossing from bank to the row of palms, crisscrossing, backwards and forwards, tumbling and stretched. By the water the Grump is standing and the eager bears cast shadows on his back. I hum their imaginary music.

Then they begin to leap like acrobats or joyful monkeys, the dying light igniting on their spiked grey brown fur. I watch them till the light dies; watch as they leap between the palms, arms outswinging; watch as they never touch each other by accident or design. I open my mouth and sing quietly, gently, unobtrusively. The sun vanishes, and, just as they arrived, the river bears melt into the darkness.

And everything seems so quiet.

If the islands go the obelisk crumbles, the birds vanish, and everyone will join the flow of busy striving that I see passing by, see their faces as they envy our singing, our sitting, our simplicity. Can the flow of striving take so many more? Is it never ending, this busy, they never sit and watch or feel the perfection of stillness? They never see the dragonfly humming, the river bears dancing and the sun-tipped water rippling with pleasure.

Shallow Shore

Sometimes they're on the shore and he can hear them and he can sense them. Sometimes they wade through the reed beds and he can hear them brushing against the fine thin leaves. Sometimes they rattle the handles of the house and rev boat engines.

When he takes the boat out at night he avoids them and heads to the middle, to the sea, and the vast horizon and the calmness of the water.

There's a child sitting in the middle of a neon green lawn, a toddler, and he is spilling out crimson sick, which fades into pale as it hits the ground. He looks marooned by his sickly spilling. His pale blue cardigan is handknitted. The man at the window stares at the child. He claws the window, shakes the frame. Gordie is a man of shadows. And the child, his son, Alexander, a fragrancy of air. When the night comes and Gordie is afflicted by sound, the revving of engines, his guilt building up into the night sky, he stares out at the sea, at the reeds rushing along his eyeline like frightened coots, and at the channels of water flashing in the night-moon dark.

Always there are birds. A floating pageant of them, blue and black waders, snowy egrets, orange black grebes with crowns and fancy headdresses. The child Alexander giggles at them as if his sounds are bubbles.

The living room looks across the estuary toward the hill where the town is. The walls aren't filled with air but the cries and cackles of wading birds. The oystercatchers in frantic panic, the plovers dipping, the sandpipers hurrying along the heavy sand, rushing for worms before the water floods in again. The water is shallow at the shore and Alexander likes to sit and play with worm-drilling cast offs.

The boy giggles, and bubbles join the geese chatter in the living room. Look, he says, daddy, look how I laugh and bubble.

Gordie paws the walls, Gordie rattles the windows, Gordie tears up the carpet leaving his son alone in the middle, an island of carpet. Stop playing with the bubbles, boy, he says.

The bubbles, the boy holds in his hands, fit like minute planets, as solid as steel.

At night the engines come again and Gordie can't sleep. He sees tankers and fishermen and strangled swans red white, bloody. He sees men running down gangways, gangways of steel. He sees crashing boats and thunder noise and the horizon lit up like a Belisha beacon. He closes his eyes, grips the pain in his legs, the steel cold pain, steel like a mortuary slab, no longer marble but manufactured in crucibles of heat. And tries to blank his mind. Tries to see channels of escape.

In the morning he finds his boat cut and slashed like business suits by a betrayed wife.

The catamaran lies akeel on the reed bank. It is all he has left now. The channels snake away from the house, he loves the slithering paths of water, the inlets and the outlets, the places where birds hide, the birds inside his green and crazy catamaran, 'Knots', the marks and shit they leave. The bits of feathers and things they bring. All birds are magpies. The sails are grimy. He can see his child crawling on the acid green grass. He can see the power station to the right heaving pouches of steam, the water pushes, a pebble lands carefully to his Wellingtons. The pebble is hot. Steam rising. He looks to the power station. The sails of the catamaran are full of mould and lichen. He tries to wipe away and leaves waves of stains along the canvas. A bell, not a chime, more an assault on the air, blasts. The power station.

Gordie tries to lift the catamaran. It's his only form of escape.

But he loves the house. And his child. Alexander is smiling. The oblivion of childhood. How can he leave?

He can't lift the boat off the reed banks. It flops down with a huge crunch. And water, cold punishing water, splashes up his legs.

At night he looks at the catamaran, its form stagnant and heavy like a beached whale, the light from the cloudy moon erratic and strident working over the white lichen sails, the white fins of the tail, the breeze running like invisible mice over it, and dreams of escaping.

He always dreams of escaping. The child coughs and cries in his sleep and the kitchen feels cold and dirty and uninhabitable and he walks back to the living room after tucking in the boy and stands again at the window looking out at the power station's luminous smoke and the catamaran and the silting channels and pulls on the curtains till the pole shifts from the rawlplug, the screw twizzles backwards and falls out of its hole, and the wooden pole tips and turns and the curtains fall and collapse.

Gordie scratches the walls. His scratching makes patterns over them, like tiger markings, clawing his way out. But his arms feel weak and the noises come again. The reeds are alive with whispers. Voices sliding through the grasses, voices on the air, voices in whispers, voices in shouts, voices with sinister cries. How do they do that? The reeds rub together, like stridulating crickets. Voices. Whispers.

The bedroom is cavernous. He cannot sleep. The child cries again and he jumps up.
In the morning Alexander smiles.

On the lawn Alexander is smiling. Acid green smiles. Smoke from the power station wanders across the river like signals. He catches the smoke, pull its drifts and twines towards him. He holds out his giggle-balloons and tries to thread the smoke through them. He says, *Where's mummy?*

49

Gordie sits on his haunches and looks to the sky before covering his face with his hands, catching smoke-signals from the power station between his skin-peeling fingers.

They make lunch, the two of them, young and old, tall and small, the son smiling up at his father as his hands get covered in melting cheese, he pulls the cheese threads between his fingers. It drips down his chest, down his red sweatshirt, spits of melted mozzarella. From buffalos, his father says, that cheese comes from buffalos.

Not cows?

When they've finished their lunch, Gordie sits him by the dining table to do drawings, while he goes out to finish cleaning and mending the catamaran.

Every day the channels seem to get wider and the reeds retreat, still growing, still taking up space but never round the house anymore. Once, where the reeds seemed to be attacking the house, they were now retreating and the channels widening, soon to vanish, letting the house float out into the estuary, into the power station sitting out there like a guarding castle. A templar castle, a conqueror's castle. Enormous walls, like huge slabs, like Mycenae.

The boy dreams of heroes running up the walls. Dreams of heroes. I am Alexander, he says, the greatest general the world has ever known. I come from blackest seas, highest mountains; no walls are too big for me to climb. Bricks and mortar submit at my feet. I charge; I run.

He paints; he draws; he dreams while Gordie cleans the instrument of his escape. He has to be ready.

A large ship prowls from the power station's profile. Slowly. He watches it through binoculars and wonders if it is the ship he was on. It looks similar. More strangers entering the town port? It begins to rain again. It's been raining for weeks. It's been raining forever, it feels. The town is drenched with water: on the rare occasions he goes into the streets' twisty roads, a maze of roads and street and tumbling battlements, for provisions, people stare at his leg as if they know it was him there that night. He feels that they know; inside his head seeing everything he's ever done, and still the rain comes down like vengeance.

He grabs at his leg, puts down the binoculars and then continues cleaning. The afternoons he spends his time keeping draughts out of the house, draughts coming through the cracking windowpanes, smoke from the power station lingering in the living room like a drunken man's breath. The walls heave and shudder, the refrigerator creaks, the table shakes, the rain pokes through holes in the walls, penetrates through the roof, creeping down the interior as silent as fruitful germs. Rain soaks the aged sofas, rain settles into the dog's basket; drops of rain running over the kitchen unit, soaking the packets of food, the rice, the noodles, the weevilled bags of flour. In the bathroom silverfish scatter when the light is put on. In the bedroom is always the smell of old unwashed women, old clothes, old breaths. Cloths hanging, women's things to fall over.

That afternoon she returns. The rain halts. She stands in the periphery of the garden like a sentinel. Dressed in green florals. Hair like twine. She's watching. When he sees her he doesn't know what to do and they stare at each other till Alexander shouts, mummy, and stumbles towards her. Her face transforms from hard to jubilant and she runs towards the boy.

Gordie backs away towards the catamaran and scrubs even harder at the lichen, trying to block out the screams and giggles and the bubbles of joy the boy creates. The ache in his leg intensifies and he can hardly move. He looks to the sky thankful for a break in the endless rain and hobbles from front to back of the boat. Front to back. The sky greys. Time passes.

She says, you should never have gone on that ship.

Cripple, she shouts as she leaves. Cripple.

The boy is gone too.

That night the sounds in the leaves return. He can even see their faces now as they slink closer, through reeds, trailing through the shallow water, frightening the sleeping coots. Faces scarred and buckled and drowned in deep-sea water, the darkest water beneath which are fish with scrunched up faces of hate. Teeth like lions. And barely breathing. Barely seeing. These fish are all teeth and hard skin. The cold is hardening at the bottom of the dankest darkest sea. He thinks of their bodies, their tiny hopeful foreign bodies floating, sinking, sleeping.

The sounds cannot be the travellers on the ship. They are *Them*, full of anger at him for letting them down. Dark faces of profit, voices of necessity than friendship. Companions of convenience.

He lets everyone down.

His son is no longer in his room crying and instead it is Gordie who lets tears come. He is a man who could blow up diamonds.

The house is white and in sunlight looks cheerful and eye-catching. The catamaran is working. He uses it to fetch Alexander from the child's mother's while the woman has her back turned chatting to people in the street. She lives in the twisty streets of town. She loves the full life of activity and companionship. The house on the estuary, stuck out with power station and reeds and egrets for neighbours, was too bleak for her. She is one of those who hates darkness, yet is full of blackness inside, cut through like seaside rock, pitch black. Gordie is sensitive to her inner void, as if it is an electric current it sparks off in him.

With the boy he glides past the power station, the boy strapped to the back and laughing and giggling his silky bubbles.

We went to a doctor's, the boy says as they climb off the boat. Gordie pats the boat as if it can breathe and needs reassurance.

I've taken you to doctors. I am always taking you to doctors. There are many doctors I can take you to.

These are different doctors, mummy says. Doctors to help me settle, she says, into what will happen. Gordie puts the boy down, allowing him to be sick.

Your mother has given up. I haven't.

He watches the boy playing on the lawn; he has a favourite toy, a plane, silver and gleaming with futuristic wings. A fox slinks out of the trees and crosses high over the back garden, watching the boy, stopping for a moment to sniff the decaying air. Then vanishes, panicked.

Sometimes, when his wife took the child before, saying he needs to rest, he needs love, he needs to prepare for what lies ahead, Gordie would leave the house. He'd travel around the area, looking at houses hidden in valleys, or houses on hills. Avoiding towns. Avoiding traffic. He'd see a house, and imagine living there and for a moment would dream of the lifestyle away from the insidious death air of the power station. He even imagined living in caves, in tents, in a van, in a mobile home, in a truck. Anything to get him away. Make his son well. Make him well. Anything but this death-existence. He would do it. He would get the money. Anything to get the money. Kill animals, sabotage experimental field crops, act as a courier, find safe houses for smuggled strangers. Anything. Anything. He looks at his son playing near the shoreline. He hates his sickness, hates his existence sometimes, hates being hemmed in, and yet can't own up to that hate.

Or he'd spend hours on the sea, looking back to the shore, looking for coves to hide in, looking for another existence as a man of the beach. But everywhere was the effluent from the power station. It was even in his head now. He could sense it just like bad smells of febrile men hiding in reeds.

He always comes back. The boy survives without him. Calls up his mother. Sometimes sits spewing sick on the lawn while counting bubbles in his hands. Bubbles in the sky like talismans, around his head. He shouts to them, aliens aliens on the green. The power station grunts and screams and the lawn shakes, the house shakes some more.

Gordie feels the itch to be gone again. To be elsewhere. To be left alone. The voices at night get closer and he knows one day they'll stop jibing him and do something to take real vengeance on him. He grips his crippled leg and thinks it wasn't his fault. The accident. Cripple, his wife called him. Cripple. Taste the effluence in his mouth, taste the sickness in his muscles. He walks away from the house. He stands at the back, high over the garden where the fox disappeared. Fox trails into wilderness.

The boy Alexander, almost standing, almost marching, stumbles closer to the shore, places a hand on the boat, caresses the soft metallic surface. White gleaming. And sits down in the water. Gordie doesn't seem to notice that the boy has moved.

Then Alexander lies back and swallows water and coughs. Lifts up his head, covered in water. Puts his head back under the water again, in small deliberate movements. Little pellucid creatures, hardly fish at all, cling to his skin. Twinned sea-moss, circles of froth, grey brown effluence. The water covers him. The froths shift over him like rain clouds over the sky. Water runs over him and into his nostrils, into his gaping mouth, soaking his purple dungarees, blue checked shirt, running inside his pale belly, whirling round his distended belly button, creeping over his legs and his small red Wellingtons. Alexander the greatest general, the man of the universe, the man to conquer continents, solve problems, is lying down in water.

Gordie turns and see him.

Gordie moves, quickly now down the hill towards the shore. Rain falls. Fast hard strips of metallic rain rushing to the chalky ground, and out to the water's edge. Rain falls on the boy's face half submerged in water.

Gordie running.

The power station screaming. A boat pulling into the town's harbour honks. The shore edge is only a few inches of water. A few inches of water. Gordie is running and rushing and racing and his crippled leg slows him. It's like he's running through a wall of mud.

Alexander's eyes are still open when Gordie reaches him, by the time he kneels down into the water to pick up the boy. His eyes staring at the clouds and the sky. He almost looks like he is smiling. Giggle bubbles. Bright blue eyes. Bright blue eyes.

It's late now. Like a dark misshapen sack Gordie sits in the catamaran imagining being on the water and out to sea, and the possibilities now before him. The vacant house is surrounded by a halo of tentative radiance.

Empty house, decaying house. He watches the reeds till the true dark comes, and hopes to trap the terrifying voices, the male bodies of voices as they rush the tumbling house, and then maybe he can be gone.

Bone on Bone

I fell in love with a pianist, with his dextrous fingers across the keyboard. Long fingers, knuckles firm and resolute under the lights, but flexible and floating like liquid across the keys. I watch him smiling to the bassist and the sax player. He has a long nose, broad mouth and when he smiles he shows all his teeth. I find that sexy in a man.

His hair is dark, his shirt white, his jacket black.

I follow the quartet around the country, up greasy deserted highways, to strange clubs in blocked off streets. I sit at the bar, a normal girl, falling in love, fingering peanuts, ignoring the barman, and tapping my foot. I had discovered the quartet by accident. One night, wandering through a deserted town, I pulled over and walked into a bar and there they were. I know their music. I know their van. I know all their haunts, and where they sleep at night.

The pianist is called Nels.

I buy them drinks; sometimes I do take my eyes from the pianist. They know me now too.

At night I dream of his fingers on my body: those knuckles, the strength, the long long fingers, pressing, playing. I dream of his fingers in my mouth, touching my ivory teeth, outlining my lips.

His playing mesmerizes me, and I am nowhere, everywhere, floating. I'm around, I fill in the spaces between the players, between the notes,

I hover above his shoulder trying to guess which note he will play next; how he reads these notes; they are like books to him, unopened books, unused words. On *Night in Tangiers* he is magician, wizard, I cannot believe where he takes me. He touches the keys and out flows a narrative. His narratives create such emotions in me: one minute I am ecstatic and rushing along in the groove, the next I am sullen, bashful. His fingers create the notes, the notes create emotions, the emotions turn me on. I cannot stop wanting him. With every note he plays – his fingers sweet, strong fluid, mercurial fingers – he makes me want him more. I am in love with his talent, with what he can do. I hear him and I am beyond everything, I am above beyond; it's like mixing with butterflies and angels, swooning with colours deep inside my head.

The streets are cold and wet. I stand in rats' alley, waiting for him. He's no famous musician, just a small-time jazzman with fingers that make me crazy.

Rain drips on my head, runs down my neck and soaks my shirt. I am still watching. Music makes me crazy. I am humming *A Love Supreme*, Coltrane, which Nels's band does so brilliantly. I am alone. There aren't thousands of screaming teenagers, just this old one. Then the lights go out in the B&B. I say goodbye to the rats and slink away.

One night between sets he speaks to me. In a voice like melted chocolate, he asks for my name. His touch on my arm makes me lie. I invent someone who has never existed.

As Serena of Beckenham I rent a hotel room, where I wait for him to visit me. I am sure he will. The sun rises. I sleep.

I am from nowhere and everywhere. I lack history. I lack passports and pensions and things that tie me to the ground. I have a real name, I have a real life but it is hidden inside me. I am no longer me.

That night at the club I go in and pretend I don't know him. He is busy. The club smells of beer, of a hundred stomping feet and sweaty players. I could vanish now and he wouldn't know who I was. I buy a hovering stranger a beer, watching the pianist watching me as he checks his keyboard; he had been smiling broadly.

I could live in a small house by the common, or a high flat overlooking the railway; I could be a social worker, a banker, a balloonist or a trapeze artist. His smile has wiped my name from within me.

Call me Serena, call me Pianissimo, call me Allegra.

Nels is playing, and just looking at him makes my skin pulsate. I am inspired; I can feel the shape of my fingers, the very skin along the bone of my nose, the muscle, the fat; everything pulsates, freckles dance, muscle pushes against skin. Soon the skin will break and I will burst. I want to reach out and touch him as he plays, to feel his fingers as he creates those notes. I sit on my stool, twiddling round and round, feeling the bubble gum under the plastic seating. The seat is red and squeaks like a kitten.

People are watching me. I am alone. My chin juts into the air; the air smells unwashed, fetid, like morning breath. The air settles on me like dust and we all smell as one.

Old men walk past on tiptoes, bellies in like drill sergeants. But they are old men and will always be so, were probably born so. Notes punctuate the air; emphatic sax, stabbing beats.

I am heightened and vain, wrapping strands of my muddy-coloured hair around my stumpy fingers. I am comfortable with my body, which I could share with the world if needed. My lust for him makes me generous. I chat to people around me, over the music, under the music and between the music. A man sits beside me, his fingers yellow, his mouth small and his hair smelling of hay.

"You look very friendly."

"Oh I am. Very friendly."

"Enjoying the music?"

I nod and look at the pianist. His hands are still as he watches me. Then it comes to his turn to play. Sinew and bone dissemble and the piano keys move as if played by liquid as his fingers skitter across them. He smiles freely.

A circle of men around me. It doesn't matter if I am attractive or not. I am open and they are like dogs.

"Need a drink?"

"I always need a drink." They fetch me drinks, they knock against me, they brush against me. Between the music, the banter flows.

"You're not from round here."

"I could be."

"I've never seen you before."

"Neither have I."

We laugh. We have pain and history and desire, friends and lost loves and offspring hidden in beds not of our choosing, but none of it matters in this darkened room with my hair stinking of beer and hope. Smoke drifts. The sax drifts. Only the pianist is strong. I cannot take my eyes from him. Someone coughs, the sax stutters, the men laugh, and in a far corner a woman leans back over the top of her chair and kisses a man.

The sweet phrasing; a jumble of notes. I close my eyes, lost again. How easily I am lost and transported like scent. Floating. That piano again. It is as if touching the keys the pianist touches some black and white ivory in me. I clench inwards. Tingle. Desire is a torturer. It stabs me. How can this longing be real, and if he touches me will I liquefy? Eyes closed, I touch him, I smell him. Each note he plays is tattooed into my flesh. I am in his fingers like bone. Bone on bone. Chords dazzle, they tease, running up and down my body, and the air is suddenly wind-fresh.

The man beside me touches me. His touch, on my thigh, is deliberate and bold. I turn round. He presses against me, runs his fingers down my arse. If a lover were standing next to me, he would look the lover in the eye while touching me. He is impertinent. I let him. Again he runs his fingers down my back, down my arse, as if following the contour of a river down a map. I am excited by this seedy encounter, but I move away, I walk into the glare of lights. The band plays: piano notes, not as good as before, but hypnotizing. I turn to look. His fingers are like eddies over the keyboards, his eyes closed. He is hovering in the music and for once I cannot join him. I feel the other man's touch still contouring my back.

It's night. Wind is screaming outside. Leaves run like children down the road. Taxis splutter. The air is full of acrid smoke from the chemical factory over the way, in the distant sodium–lit glare. I close the window and wait. The hotel I have booked is opposite theirs, and I have made sure they saw me entering the building.

I am waiting, and planning all the things I will tell him about myself: I will show him my moles, the scars on my knees. I will tell him about falling from swings as a child. I will tell him how I want to live in New York and drive taxis, how I see angels when I am sick.

Only with him will I become solid. I will say my favourite colour is indigo, my favourite word frazzle, I dream of ravines and white water, and of owning clubs in slick city streets. I will tell him how I like to drive fast cars round abandoned rural airports, drive them so fast I almost defy gravity. My friends tell me I have a talent for melodrama. But I will tell him all: the history, the lowdown, my dreams, other lovers who leave me dry, other men I have loved and lost.

He visits me dry and shiny from a gig. His lack of sweat is part of his charm. He removes his jacket. His white shirt is almost pristine. The hotel room is vibrant blue. A picture of a man smiling at us on the wall. I take his jacket and fold it. The music in my head wraps around him and he is playing. As I touch him, I can see and hear him playing, the notes are vibrant, the notes dance and I am thrown up into the firmament.

I take him to the bed, I touch his lips, they part sweetly as if expecting chocolate. His shirt unbuttoned, his chest white, his face is intent and serious but his lips smile. That I want him so much is like a power surge through his body.

He sleeps now.

Days pass in a white hotel bed: crumbs on the sheets, spunk stains vanishing each afternoon. We are hidden in the bed, like exiles. He doesn't play his piano. He is engrossed in my visions of angels, in my favourite words and colours that I wrap round his head like tinsel. He loves what stories I give him of a world he cannot imagine.

It is easy to divert him, beguile him, even. Now when he should be practising, or turning up for rehearsals, he is instead flexing his fingers on me. He plays me sublime and I am created whole from notes in his hands. "Your body is soft," he says, "whereas the piano is hard. You are more pliable than ivory."

Hidden deep in white sheets we play, while the light changes outside.

When we sleep together he hums.

We are almost too perfect.

Finally we leave for another grimy town, and another dark hotel back room where a handful of serious enthusiastic people come to hear them play. I distract him. My presence, instead of enlivening, suppresses him. It's as if by walking around the room, passing from bar to bar, catching the eye of others, my dark hair flashing red under the lights, I inhibit him. His playing is stiff, like his fingers are stuck together with glue. He plays; they clap. I clap; I am vociferous in my appreciation. He plays again. He gets into the groove, he finds the groove; oh look at him smile. I adore his smile. It fills his face. Eyes closed. The room is with him.

So quiet apart from the sax and the bass and the piano. Drums come in. We're hypnotized and teased; we wait for the next notes to take us away. Someone coughs. A man in a red jacket shuffles away. I look at my nails for dirt, and then he plays again and the notes are exquisite diamonds. Suddenly he looks at me and loses it. The notes wither away from him like falling leaves. The keys are closed, the narratives gone. He presses fingers to bone.

He comes to me. "I was crap tonight," he says. I comfort him. "Tomorrow you will be better," I say.

At the next gig he is lacklustre. People leave, straying away to other gigs, other bars. I sit at the front still breathing in the sax and its snake-like notes whizzing up my spine. The bass awes me and the drums inspire me.

The pianist is quiet. The chords he discovers in his keys are dull and mundane. I feel sorry for him.

In cheap hotel rooms, finally I tell him my name. In cheap hotel rooms
we dream and plan futures. I touch him and he is full of life. I take his
fingers and make them sing. Bone on bone, flesh touching me. When
he's inside me I touch music; I have stolen his music.

He tries to play. He hangs out with his band and smiles and says,
"Today, I will be amazing." But his fingers clunk and the notes trip over
one another. The piano is alien to him. So now, he avoids the band and
stays with me. He knows that when we touch his music returns. Without
me he is empty and lifeless.

I go to gigs now without him, but feverish with Nel's music within me.
I watch sax players and am transformed. I hear piano players playing
chords that Nels should be playing, discovering his stories, sending me
places I love to go, while Nels sits inside and watches the leaves twist a
path down the damp streets, and waits for me.

I am in love with a pianist; without his piano what is he?

More Moments of Sheer Joy

Islands are like moments; sheer moments of joy in water. Tiny perfections lasting a finite time; situated in a particular space and occupying the ecstasy side of the brain. The more moments you have the more you want. Just like islands. One is rarely enough.

I wonder if you can get addicted to the things.

The boat, approaching the island, an iridescent mass of shellac, green and blue in the ocean, clunks to a stop. Waves sting at my hands. Another island waits for me. The boat rocks; the boatman steadies himself. A breeze lifts from the water and runs through my hair with a lover's touch. I look at the boatman opposite as he steers. He is so tanned, so healthy-looking.

I can smell the island. Smell its limits; sense its end and sheer joy of completion. An island, no matter its actual shape, is like a circle. It completes and surrenders itself. It is perfection composed of granite, earth and sand. I set foot on an island and am infused with joy like a religious ecstasy.

I am waiting for the moment to begin. The boat swerves, the man, silent, weather-mocked, pointed ears like they'd been wind-bitten, tries hard to keep it still. Children, like small mannequins, brightly coloured and shoeless, just like in the Sunday Supplements, race to the pier; sounds

The Cusp of Something

of thumps on wooden-slatting, bright smiles, laughter, tiny hands. Around them annoying insects flit over small, distended puddles in sand. The air exotic, warm, consuming.

I am not alone.

Back on the main ferry I saw a man. Just an ordinary man, hair the colour of sodden matchsticks, face delicately shaped like fragile wax mouldings, legs thin and elegant like a tango dancer, bending over, tying up his shoelaces and then he knocked his head on the railing and smiled sheepishly at me, looking quite silly. His smile made me ache. I decided then it was time I had an affair. I didn't ache for him in particular: more a general ache for fresh faces, fresh skin, and moments in my body to match the exquisite islands. I remembered my husband then, for a moment.

You leave me parched. I lie spread out before you, your semen dribbling down my thigh. Everything about me is vulnerable and more honest than any moment in my life. If you would but look. Look at me, I want to scream, *look at me*. Can't you see now is when I want you? Now! Don't leave me like this. You think I am done just because you are? My head bent towards your toes, my back bending away from your head, you lying flat beneath me, my hips uplifted, my body expectant. This is me. I have moved for you. I have tried every trick I know and still you finish. Oh so satisfied. Read me, just read me. Read the words of my body, read the contours, the shapes I am making. I make these shapes for you. For me. For us both. I stretch out my arms before me – it triangulates me – and lift my hips slightly away from you, my cunt contracting as if grasping for air or flesh; my body would beg if it could say the words. I shape the words... I want to feel you so much, feel you against me and inside me. I wait, pressing down on my hands. I wait. You've not seen, you've not guessed I need more touch than what you've given me. You think that's it. I wait still. You lift up your leg, you smile, I move away, you kiss me. You are happy and wordless. You leave me parched.

The first step onto the island is always the most important. Someone takes a picture of me and I smile. A practised smile. I shake hands with

64

important people. Large hands. I say how happy I am to be here in this tropical paradise. They tell me what I will see: waterfalls, lakes, rivers, interiors of excellent schools, hotels for exotic carefree tourists. I move up dark-tiled stairs and into a white and yellow hotel room, an anonymous shower and coolness on my body. Water drenches me. Yellow tile patterns on the wall, making the image of a fat box.

The first island was cold, and off Norway: Bolga – far north, a small island, freezing water everywhere, with views of other islands: Storvika, Åmnøya, Meløy. My intent is to avoid the major islands, as I said in my press release. Just minor islands; islands off islands. They asked me how long it would take. I said a year. They asked how my husband felt about me being absent so long. I said it was for charity. He understood. He agreed with what I was doing. He could join me on any island. It didn't need to be a lonely sojourn. He was welcome any time. Now I am glad I am alone. I have been doing this for five months three weeks and five days, and possibly forty minutes. This is island number 14 or is it 15? Norway and then Bornholm, Elba, Sicily – including smaller islands off; islands caught in a day sweep round the coast, like fish in a net, – Malta, then Greece which was a dream. I wandered around the Cyclades like Odysseus.

Yet I yearn to see Zanzibar: a place strangely exotic, unknown; to walk the Stone Town with the scent of cinnamon in my hair, sleep with the aroma of cumin on my pillow, enclosed in the drifting scent of cloves on the night air: somewhere completely unreal. Impossible, yes.

Sponsors give me money for mentioning their products everywhere I go, for the publicity I get for them and for each island I visit. Sometimes islands give me gifts and money, though I usually leave them with armfuls of sponsors' products. On Karos, in the Cyclades, I was given a donkey, which I had to leave behind. Good publicity usually breeds more money. The time the ferry sank off the coast of Turkey, and I had to pull in unexpectedly into southern Cyprus, brought me in more money than I could ever dream of. I pledged I would raise a million, when I've reached that figure I can go home. How many more islands before then?

On Maderia I caught chickenpox after my lucky Buddha fell into the water. It was small, shiny red and much touched, for reassurance, and now it's in the harbour water, run over by fishing boats and pleasure cruisers. On Madeira a French man in a dark suit smelling slightly of petrol and coffee walked over to me and we talked. He walked me into an alleyway. I was scared. I smiled at him. He reached his hand towards my neck, resting behind me on the wall, pinning me from escape. He was pretty in a grown up sort of way. Pretty and charming with grey hair. I could have just let him finger me, at least. I wish I had. I wasn't ready then.

The islands seem to be getting smaller. I've been to medium islands and then large ones – avoiding the really big country islands, continent islands, such as Australia, Japan, and now back to intimate islands. How many islands are there in the world? Has anyone ever counted? And Asia is like one big splodge surrounded by hundreds of lesser dots. Now on the smallest of the British Virgin Islands, fearing that when I get to Polynesia I may slip off the edge of an island and vanish into the ocean. I could spend my life doing this and never go back. This place is truly paradise. Oh such horseshit clichés. But just look at it. I don't want to leave. There is only one other thing I would need to keep me here. What is my life in England to compare to here?

A yacht moves into focus, pulling in for the night. A big yacht. Four sails in a beautifully symmetrical pattern, like dancers. The yacht glides in, like Arthur's boat floating to Avalon. Just two people on the beach. Can a place be more unreal? My footsteps on the wooden-slatted balcony confirms its physicality. How is it that some people get to live in such a place? Endless bougainvillea round the door, clean white floors, a balcony view overlooking deep green hills and the ocean. The endless ocean. Down below is the beach: fine, wide, empty. This is a tiny island. I could go snorkelling, scuba diving. I've never had sex underwater! I don't need to ever leave. I think I am going to cry or die or blow up fat like Big Daddy. Become an eccentric Welsh woman gone mad under the sun, drinking mint juleps by the ferry load. Here I could have a lover who fucks me in daylight, on the beach, under trees, spreading my body over a rock, water at my feet, sun burning me, his body over me, in me. We'd meet casually on hot street corners and run to a sheltered spot, brushing over reaching bougainvillaea from our faces. I'd feel alive and wanted. I'd feel alive.

Here I am. Alone, doing almost exactly what I want to do at this moment. All the books say you should do what liberates you. It says listen to your inner voice. It tells me what I want. It tells me I have to look after number one: (*"and number one is you -! Yeah!"*) What happens when bolstering your self-esteem hurts others?

I send you a postcard from here, portraying big fluffy clouds, blue sky, azure waters – the whole caboodle of clichés. I send you a postcard from every island I go to. They are pictures of the world I now inhabit. Of course you have the photos people take and the sponsors keep you informed and you see me in the press – once placed just inside the front page to now hiding further and further into the back pages; no doubt you'll expect to see me on the tiny gossip pages soon enough! Do you expect me to fail? I think you do. I send you love and kisses and describe what I see. Indeed I do love you. Sometimes I even miss you.

You deserve the best.
Both of us can't deserve the best when the best is conflicting.

Once I had a lover who knew how to treat me. Many lovers, even, before I met my husband. Lovers who knew their way joyfully around a woman's body; lovers who excelled teasing and taunting and licking my clit; lovers who lingered, and lovers who knew when to be aggressive, when my body needed force and when I needed delicate beautiful tentative strokes inside me, who knew when to turn me round, how to touch me inside to make me squeal and leap from the bed in amazement, touching the ceiling with the thrill of it all; lovers who would caress me with words and music and wine, as well as the power of who they were. Lovers who were certain of themselves. I miss that. It's been a long time.

I remember Zeb, who would spend hours with me, whole afternoons, in a sun-drenched room, central heating way up, wandering the Victorian flat naked, drinking wine, talking, dancing energetically to

Cuban music on the stereo. His speciality was to make sure I'd come at least three times before he did. He had seduced me when I was 19. His body shone. He was fit, young and toned. I loved running my hands over his body, having him caressing my thighs, stroking me, looking at me, telling me I could do anything I wanted. Filling me with confidence from his sure touch. He would kiss my thighs, kiss my labia, kiss every part of me, loving the taste of my juices in his mouth. I loved those sun-soaked hot winter afternoons.

I take a trip on a sleek yacht, polished, chromed, and efficient like an ideal robot. I tie back my unruly hair – a mass of maddening brown curls, and thrust my bikini-clad body into the sun. We land on an uninhabited rocky island where my host and I stride about the barren place like conquerors. He's tall with an Irish voice, blue eyes and wrinkles from too much sun; too much sailing round the world, and is a master of harbours and islands and weather conditions. He cooks exquisite cleanly sharp meals on a tiny hob and I marvel at the minute space he inhabits physically and the infinite space he roams mentally. I think it would be good for him to touch me. I look at his thin bony freckled hand. Those fingers that untie knots so deftly. I smile at him.

The sand is hot. The speckled rocks are hot, covered with vibrant insects. The air is full of them and the sound of birds. I watch the small boat bobbing, tucking my legs under me, admiring the depth of tan I am acquiring.

Island no. 16. I hope someone has taken a picture. I shout to the guy left on the yacht, over the small chasm of water, "Hey get the camera! Take a picture of me! I need proof!"

Without proof I cannot get the money. All those corporate sponsors and their tax-deductible donations, garnering free publicity and great PR. Look, they care about African Orphans, Disappearing Cheetahs, Research into Cystic Fibrosis. The charity I'm doing this for right now is for gorillas and orang-utans.

Where do you start choosing who is the most deserving? I began with my distaste for the trouble humanity embroils itself in – even though it may not be each individual's absolute fault, and my love for an old toy orang-utan I had when I was eight called Herbert – and picked an animal charity. You have to start somewhere.

Is there really anything more worthwhile to life than passion? Without it what are you?

We are alone on the island; exploring red-sand cliffs, red the colour of the evening sun, exploring the edge of the water, the tide-marks, the rock pools, the inner oasis, the greenness of the ground past the soft sand. I laugh uncontrollably when, standing under the cliff, he asks to sleep with me. He doesn't touch. He doesn't reach down to me, my back rubbing against the hard rock, to touch my cheek, or pull down a fragile bikini string, or unravel my hair from its loose tie, but instead he looks at me as if I am immobile, and says, "Rachael, let's lie down under this rock and make love." Without touch it is simple to refuse. When actually I want the authority of touch on me, skin on skin. There is nothing like it. Not even islands can compete. He brushes against me in the yacht. I lean against him so one breast presses against his arm. But he does nothing. He uses his voice when I want his skin. I wish I could say yes. Zeb would be able to seduce me easily.

It's empowering to go for your dreams

I have a strong fantasy life. Sometimes I take refuge in there for hours at a time, especially at night, or alone in my bed in the morning. I am like teenager imagining her first kiss. I don't caress my arm, but if it wasn't so silly maybe I would. Sometimes what I imagine frightens me but it's only thoughts and dreams.

People on the island ask about my life at home in England. I have a strange English accent, they say. I laugh and say that's because I'm Welsh and grew up outside Hay on Wye, a town of bookshops where literary men come once a year to pontificate. We've had presidents, ex-presidents, famous novelists bothered by controversy like wasps on a summer's afternoon. Now I live in Canterbury, a town of sacrifices and martyrs. The town is a martyr to tourists. See how it subjugates itself. Henry II would adore it.

They ask about children. They are sweet, these islanders. Some incomers are runaways from America. The hotel owners are obviously gay. Their cooking is superb: shrimp so fresh, so tender and crisp, I swear I saw it out in a small rock pool just hours earlier.

I say I have one child, Elissa, with her speech impediment and fascination for insects. She is six – the same age as my marriage. Doesn't she miss you? Oh yes, I imagine. Don't you miss her? Indeed, more than you can know, but I have to do this. Sometimes I wonder how I could have left her. But she is safe with my husband. It is only for a year.

My mind is like a black box whose hinged lid you have no way of lifting. It used to embarrass me. The dreams I could see. Daylight with you makes me bashful. There, I am no one a friend would recognize. I am no one daylight would greet with familiar smiles. Now I can truly let my inhibitions fall away like coverings. I can dream openly of what I want, now I am away from you. I can imagine a lover who explores my body, who takes time and care, who has fingers that probe and delve and search and liquefy. A man to whom I could shout aloud 'Fuck me' without it sounding silly, to whom I could invite into my ass without fear or trepidation of reaction. A man who could pull my nipples and bite me and tease my clit with his strong teeth. A man whose hands would firmly, delicately grab my throat as I was about to come. A man who could wrap me in soaking sheets and pull me to him. I dream of such freedom. I don't know when it changed or was it you that changed? All I want to do is marry the world of imagination with daylight. Is that so wrong? And I will do so but without you.

"Rachael! Rachael! Rachael" Children and parents are shouting and waving. The boat pulls away. They have covered me with cerise and white flowers. Big white petals with cerise spots like dribbled blood. Flowers fall on the quayside as if I am a wedding departure. This is all too much: I am only a small businesswoman with a flair for spotting talent, for spotting an idea and going for it. I am no goddess, I want to shout to them. All I did is come to your island, bring reporters and cameras and leave again. I didn't even fuck! My flair is flawed.

Airports and dry hotel rooms. I am an expert at quayside tasteless coffee and at keeping my sweet tooth amused with fat Snickers bars and popcorn in a packet, while waiting. I come ashore on America, like a seasonal tornado. I miss my moments. I miss my islands already.

There is something about the limitations of islands. Pure pleasure whereas the mainland seems infinite and thus the pleasure diffused. Some islands are long and thin, some curl round and touch its other side. Some are two but called one. Some are literally dots and one big wave would swallow them. Some are mountainous. Some are windblown and empty.

What your life is now is unacceptable; not good enough. Take control. Say it to yourself and you will be convinced.

We all need more moments of sheer joy. What is the point of it all without it? The bathroom here has flaking yellow wallpaper. I can see homes of spiders and cobwebs round the windows. I sit on the toilet, sit and think of tomorrow: of Martha's Vineyard, Nantucket. Sometimes I just decide to call in on an island on the spur of the moment. I see a name on a map and I want to go there. Islands in Chesapeake Bay look interesting... or the islands down the coast from Savannah. Are there are any countries that don't have islands at all?

I stare at maps to give me answers. I love just figuring out how an island once fitted, slotted in like a jigsaw to the mainland. I do that at night when everyone has gone to bed and my feet ache and the lights are low and I pool light over my map and my malt whisky and I lie naked on the bed, if I'm somewhere hot. It's hot tonight. Mainland America. I miss Europe; its smallness, odd customs, like driving on the right side of the road, like saying the word curtains, and posting something instead of mailing. People here are rather too friendly. Not a surly voice in the lobby. Even the press ask me nice questions. Rachael Driscoll comes to America, like some otherworld circus clown.

How big this place is – I have a map open now. Even the mainland is composed of islands: Manhattan, Staten Island, Long Island. Florida isn't real. Is it? It sticks out the bottom like a monkey's tail. Night falls. The hotel is quiet. It's hot. Unbearably hot. The air-conditioning makes too much noise. I shall never sleep. I have with me, on the side cabinet, as I do wherever I go, my wedding photo in a small metal frame, a plastic purple beaker covered with white daisies that Elissa gave me for water. The bed is yellow. Cowardice.

Change your reality.

I do not know much about the man who is helping me now, only that his name is Daniel and he interests me. Everything thrills me, even this clean harbour here on the west coast of America; I raced through islands like a baby suckles milk, and now we are preparing for the islands off Los Angeles, and then Guadeloupe and then Polynesia. I am resigned, almost to never seeing Zanzibar, which feels like the end of the world. I say to Daniel, "It's got to be the end of the world, how many other islands have two z's in them? Do you even know where it is?" He hums and ahs and guesses. "Wrong coast of Africa," I say.

It's September; we are short of a million by just £100,000.

You seem very far away from me now. I don't even know if you exist, even though you sent me a letter and here it is on my bed waiting for me unopened. I guess you'll tell me the summer is over in England, before it even begun. I guess you're going to tell me Elissa wants new trainers, or braces, or wants to stay up all night to watch MTV. You'll be saying in these fragments of news that I should come home. You'll never tell me so openly. But that's what you think. You'll say the garden misses my touch and should you paint the kitchen in yellow? And your mother has to go into hospital and your father wants to buy a new car even though he's nearly eighty. Your boss is driving you mad. I can guess all these things. I can't even begin to tell you want I am thinking, that I do not miss your touch. I want touch. But not yours and yet there is an inexplicable bond between us still, it is as if you planted a spirit within me, that watches and holds me tight, constricting all movement but thought. Am I haunted? I am not looking for love, I say. Rest assured. I don't want fissure. I just want to be reached where you cannot reach me. I am a selfish woman. Is it your spirit in me that stops me being truly uninhibited? I am moral; it is tearing me apart.

More moments. Never to see Zanzibar. It is too far away, and my time is nearly up. I fret at it. I look it up on the Internet. I stare at its shape on the map. I point it out to Daniel beside me. I have discovered that he is from Boston originally, his accent is kind of quaint and tortured, and sometimes I cannot understand him. He has trouble with my Welsh vowels and so I tone them down just for him. He cannot understand my fascination with Zanzibar. I say its name over and over again: Zanzibar. It speaks of myth, dreams, spices, fragrance, and Arabs. It speaks of something unattainable. We touch accidentally over the map of Africa. I can smell him, sense him imagine him touching me. I lean towards him. I wonder if he's a caring empathetic lover, and how his mouth will feel on my mouth. He rests his hand on mine as I point out the coastline of Zanzibar on the map. *I have to go there!* I shout, looking at pictures then appearing on my laptop screen. Coconuts, cloves, little islets, the House of Wonders, Aldabra turtles, five hundred and sixty carved doors.

"Sublimation is a dangerous thing." He says to me with so much understanding I feel like shouting. I look at him. He touches my shoulder. He pulls on my hair. My cunt wants him so badly I almost am not me.

"You sound like a self-help book."

I decide on Mexico instead of Guadeloupe. Mexican islands; there must be others. Daniel accompanies me smelling of cinnamon and ginseng shampoo. I am in a boat travelling down the length of Baja California, stopping off at islands with beautiful Spanish names. Cameras capture me climbing onto the island of Margarita, smiling. My last island. Daniel tells me, enthusiastically, how the name of California came about, from some Spanish guy's book.

It's not Zanzibar. The world doesn't come to an end. They take their last photos; I am a success; they leave me alone with one New Englander who is holding my hand delicately, and a dozen Mexicans in light clothing watching me. It feels so alien. We have the million pounds for the furry creatures. I have to return home. Rachael Driscoll returns home in triumph.

The wind gets up. Plankton float past. Mosaic water glints and washes. We head back to the boat, stand on the water's edge. I make sure the spirit of my husband is left in land, on Margarita with the children and the trees. After all I am so far from home. This place is so unreal, surely the rules don't apply here? Surely now I can take a moment from my marriage, from my promises and have just one moment for me? Daniel's hand holds onto mine even harder. He turns and begins to unbutton my shirt. The sun hits my breasts. I glance up into the sky looking at the sun, feeling heat, seagulls flying, sounds of wind in exotic trees. Heat on my breasts as he runs his hands over them, cups them. Everyone is gone. There is just us on the water's edge, his head bends down. I can see his dark hair. I touch his hair as his lips wrap round a nipple and firmly begin to pull softly between the very white edges of his teeth.

He lifts up and smiles and removes my sarong, my shirt and my underwear. I stand naked, water on my feet. He looks at me and smiles again and puts one finger between my legs. I spread. For a few minutes I close my eyes as he fingers me. Abruptly he stops, takes my hand leads me back across the wooden-slatting into the boat. No sounds on the boat. No one here at all. Just seagulls in the sky, and heat.

Lost in the moment, eyes closed breathing hard, lost in the moment the island purple mosaics flashing tunnels inside outside going through hands gripping feel your breath. The blue sea the sheer blue sea, islands that kiss like crabs, the swaying boat-deck, the sound of gulls. Wet wood beneath my feet. He touched my breast his lips, his hands, his pinching fingers his fingers inside me naked now his mouth and tongue between my legs, he holds my back, holding me with the palm of his hand, stopping me from swaying from falling – I can feel his concern for my body with every touch. This exultation of touch is what I needed. The caress of his cock, the feel of it. He pushes me to the floor with the force of his body. He says nothing but I can feel his breath on me. The mad touch he's inside me now. I'm on the deck, legs spread out no shame no embarrassment he's looking down at me he holds his cock – I love that – a man proudly holding out his cock, pushing now inside of me, riding me like this is all he has thought about since we met. I can feel and feel it and its beautiful breakthrough I can't believe I can't believe is there anything more than this? Best feeling air kissing skin clouds as voyeurs stranded spirits catching up with me.

I am on the sofa. The key in the door. He is home. I open my eyes, close my legs, jump up to meet him, and smile, scattering mementoes: cloves and maps.

Mad Angels

I'm hoping it's finally all over when he yells once more. "Don't think you'll get by without me."

Maybe I will. Maybe I won't. Looking at me, his face all stretched by adrenaline, eyes excited like rippling water – he makes me sick; maybe I'll tell him to go fuck himself.

He stops quickly as if grabbing my thoughts into his head, then turns away, to stroll, his legs kicking out, long and elegant, back out the door with Spade, before stopping to shout, "Fucking lazy cunt."

Out I go then, running out the door tripping after their imprints have vanished. Big gig that night. I'm on the guest list. I'm thought of. I'm expected. Even if I wasn't I'd push in. I push through crowds, as if they were layers of marshmallow.

Crazy Pete hands me the amyl bottle. He watches as I lift it to my nose and inhale quickly, and he laughs at me as my eyes bulge, and I feel dizzy as if I've swallowed too quickly, bubbles shooting up my nose. They say, "What you gonna do, Gail, what you gonna do?" I've told Michelle – she of the sexy rubber clothes and the death-black hair – about Phil's threats, about the way he hits me, making sure no one sees the bruises on my belly – chest – legs – ears. About how he fucks me with hatred, about how just two hours before that godforsaken evening he had raped me. Of course they don't believe me. They don't believe he could do such a thing, nor believe how he needs to control me, to keep me in check, to punish me for my imperfections, to make himself feel good.

Annie, standing next to her, just looks at me, her mascara smudged in the corner of her wonky eye, and smiles that fucking crescent-smirk-grin of hers that tells me she thinks I'm an arse. I may well be. But it ain't for her to say. I want to wipe that smile off her face. Her make up is plastered like pebble-dashing on her face. She's small and wears a Dusty Springfield fake fur coat. In fact, looking at her eyes, her hair, it's so Dusty – it's uncanny.

The band strolls to the stage, begins playing jerkily, and we mosh together, shoulders leaning into each other, stomping on toes, singing, shouting, screaming for more, hands in the air hands round bodies everyone moving like primitives, feet bruising and noses bursting with air. At one point Crazy Pete loses his hat in the crowd and dives in and brings it out like some prize. Fucking awful prize. It's squashed, torn and looks like a leftover chip wrapper. He looks funny without his hat. Not so handsome. How bald he's going, how patty, shiny, glistening like an oiled seal. Danny the van man grabs my top and tries to pull it down, not really being lewd, just overcome. I'm taking a breather and standing by the speakers when all of a sudden the guitarist – who kinda fancies himself as Keith Richards, I mean Keith fucking Richards, disgusting all bad teeth and attitude – comes charging across the stage clanging his guitar like it's some falling off part of his clapped-out old banger, and kisses me right on my mouth! I'm too shocked to move. The guitarist does this to another girl who wilts against the speakers, and I'm left motionless, a wet patch spreading across my lips like the trail of an octopus.

I wipe it off and grin wildly at Pete who is jumping up and down completely out of sync as the band goes crazy and the lights strobe as everything blurs as my head, rockets and jets into nothing. Here I'm smiling, I'm smiling!

Later at the club Pete is half asleep, clutching the amyl nitrate bottle, mouth lolling open – someone shoves in a joint like a lollipop but it just hovers there – half-in, half-out his mouth for ages – until someone filches it. He is bound to die of an overdose one day. As inevitable as air.

Phil turns up while I'm turned away from the door. Michelle alerts me by nodding her head, but I already knew he was there; intuition or something, the smell of his arrogance, crashing into the room, arrogance tinged with fear. At the gig I was safe. I could breathe, be me, what's that fucking song? – *I feel free?* Now Annie is repeating words I can barely make out but I have heard them before. "You two were made for each other. Don't you think, Michelle; Gail and Phil? Gail and Phil?" she giggles, and it's such a palpably ridiculous statement and such a pathetic inept smile, I just stare back at her blankly. They think he's charming, which sometimes he can be. How I need more poppers, how I need to be spaced out of away from here. How the fuck can we be made for each other? His eyes on me.

When I see a man with brown dreadlocks, and blue jean jacket, long legs stuffed in tight denims I freeze; in the high street, in a club, the supermarket wheeling between the fruit aisles and the confectionary, there I stop, dead in my tracks, life is paused, like frozen yoghurt. I barely breathe. I shake. They say that black men are worse on their women than white; how true this is, who can say? Girlfriends say it is. Go out with a black man at your peril; they got no respect for white women; any white woman who goes with them must be trash. Sometimes I remember their words. And black women – black women hate us and tell us all the time that black men only like to fuck us to get their own back on white men. Any guy can fuck with you – no matter their colour.

I must get rid of the fucker. When he raped me I cried almost dry tears, as dry as my cunt. It was punishment, that's what he said. Punishment for going against him all the time. He is so good that Phil, so fucking good. Never did anything wrong his entire fucking life. Blonde Danny, all badly-bleached floppy hair and wide boy smile – like that prat from the Moody Blues – all whiter shade of fucking pale crap – pinches my arm and drags me out to dance. Phil watches from the side, I can feel him chewing down the end of his joint like it is his baby blanket. At night, he likes to line up his joints, ready and waiting for the morning, like virgins on his fucking bedside table. He rolls them up and places them in a line. Most nights he does this. No one would believe a man like that would be so precise. I have felt his precision, that maniacal deftness.

I dance with Danny. Spade comes up, whispers something in his ear and Danny bows to me like a Japanese geisha girl – shit that man fancies himself! And goes with Spade to the bar. I am left in the middle of the dance floor gyrating to Black Uhuru. At Glastonbury last year in the rain and the mud the blues tent playing dub reggae all night was the only thing that kept me from hypothermia. Fucking Phil had forgotten to bring a fucking tent! Sly and Robbie, bass and drums bass and drums swaying. I will pay later for Danny dancing with me. Phil looks at me, he knows I will pay.

Dawnette walks past me then. I want to ask her about black men, black women but she has her red lips pursed. She's small, determined, beautiful, always moving like a piston in some tiny locomotive engine, always coming in from some strange part of town that I can't fathom how to reach. I can't get to her in time and she's gone. I watch who she moves up to. Some big guy. Italian, sharp grey suit – typical. I recognize him from somewhere else. She reaches up to him – he's so much taller than her – and slaps his unexpectant face and walks away quickly. I want to laugh. Someone does laugh. Everyone watches Dawnette stride out. God, that girl has balls. Wish I had more balls more often.

I don't speak to Phil at the club. He never dances, he just stands in a corner gassing. He could gas for England. Sometimes I have to talk to myself, otherwise I'd go nuts for good conversation.

There's a fight on one of the staircases. Everyone goes up to the roof. Heavy feet clanking on metal stairs. Phil looks at me, all excited and yet fearful. A crowd follows onto the flat roof, high over the warehouse part of town. From where you watch the buses squeal into the city centre with its pigeons, men carrying libations in brown paper bags, and the gaudy shops full of tosh that no one really wants to buy, yet they make themselves. Phil goes up too. I bugger off. Head for the chippy before it shuts and grab a taxi home.

I'm told later someone is pushed off the top. Or did they jump? Hells Angels came at them and thrashed this guy till his jaw broke, until his pal jumped off the roof to get away from the shafts of steel, shiny, swinging. Just mad Angels out for the night bashing up trendies. They close the place down after that. Friday nights after the pub will never be the same again.

I'm dancing at a salsa live event at the art house club: I get everywhere, me: down with the Blues, over the warehouse with the ravers, and out here in the arthouse-trendy world where everyone looks clean and healthy and full of middle-class angst in their turtle neck black jumpers and fat coats that are big enough to steal the whole of Woolworth's in. I dunno who I'm with best, really. I've even been known to posh it up for the slick and mean scene down at the canal clubs where drinks cost you double they do elsewhere. I am happier at home in the part-time whorehouse I reckon, reclining on velveteen, note that – not velvet but fake velvet – boudoir chairs whose once golden tassels have been cut or ripped off and covered in ancient spunk. But I'm dancing here and Phil never normally dances but here he is with his arms around my waist, with his arms above his head, with his hands on my arse. He is smiling. I am uneasy. What does he want? I dance with him, feeling the relief of his easy smile. Everything is going well. Today could be a good moment between us.

Someone pushes past me. A girl with red lips and white white dress, from Vivienne Westwood. I recognize it. Phil looks at her. She looks at Phil. He stops shifting his hips from side to side. He looks at her legs as she vanishes into the parting swaying movements of people falling over, tumbledown heads, unsyncopated legs. She throws back her big hair and smiles at me. And then her blonde hair is surrounded by many brown heads of lesser sophistication. Only occasionally do we get a glimpse of her star-like brilliance in the gloom, picked out by foxy radiant lights, as she stops and starts heading through the dancers like a gorgeous bulldozer. Phil's hands rest on my hips less passionately than before.

But he has claimed me for the night. I try to evade him by leaving by the backdoor after a quick bog sortie, reaching home before him.

Two hours later he breaks into the flat. I can't control how he enters my home but he doesn't really live here, not any more. I try blocking him out but he always comes back. I wake hearing the noise of him coming through my barricades, pushing down my inept attempt to stop him from getting in. I get up and find him in the living room brushing down his shirt. He smiles at me. Says nothing, motions me back into my room. I climb back into bed. He takes up residence in the chair opposite the bed. I sit up and watch him light up, watch him taking a long slow drag and staring at me deliberately. He's wearing the leather jacket I bought for him for his birthday. Even in this light I can tell how good he looks in it. I clutch the duvet around my naked torso and kick the bottom end down into place to cover my legs. His cigarette makes smoke. A van with a dodgy fanbelt passes outside. Lights from the pub across the road finally go out. I can hear wind. He says nothing. I say nothing. I prepare for rapid movement. My flesh tenses for violence.

Eventually after hours of silence at shop-opening time he asks me to fetch him fags. I smile warily and leave the flat to return shaking with a fresh packet of 20 B&H, which I pass to him. He tucks it inside his coat pocket, says thanks quietly and leaves. Smile or scream? I shake as I patch up my barricades before collapsing into bed.

It's so fucking cold I could turn into a sparkling Christmas representation of an icicle. The ground outside yet another club glistens like Phil's oil, the stuff that I have to comb gently into his afro. Gently, otherwise he shouts at me for being a clumsy cow. A tender scalp he has, like a baby's. We stand stomping our feet and clapping our hands like circus seals. Waiting. We're always waiting. Always waiting on someone, probably Annie – yes Annie, there she is, blowing kisses to the bursting bodyguards like some drag queen. "Fucking get a move on will ya, tight-arsed git!" Spade shouts and Danny laughs and stubs out his fag. Pete, staggering and almost blind in the dark, passes us, shouts, "Night, Gail!" Someone comes up to Danny and they head away into the corner laughing and huddling close – two heads into dark nit candidates. The road is shiny like a skating rink. Out there away from me nothing moves. The road is reflective like god's mirror, like the star's looking glass. I pull my fingers crack my joints and sigh. I daren't yell but I want to yell. I want to yell like I want to drown out every bit of noise that ever existed – every shout, every bell, car engine, every dog bark, every loud voice shouting at me in anger. Instead I watch the non-movement on the steps. I head out into the dark. I stand in the centre of the road and begin my walk as if the centre of the road is a tightrope. Step slightly 2AM crazy pissed stepping one foot carefully here I giggle my boots crunch against the glass-like ice that has descended onto the tarmac like a pearl fishermen's net. I know they'll follow me haphazard not careful like me they will crack the glass make noise. I step carefully I twist my foot to walk like a cat I would crouch down but they'd laugh one foot in front stretch out my leg like a poxy ballerina. Ballerina dancing on ice I throw my head up and I feel I am crunching the stars stars at my head glass ice cubes ice pinches my skin I need more Danny pops his arm around my waist. A practised movement that. He does that to hundreds of waists all over the country. Arm around waist comforting we pass shops he's dancing with my movements as if we're tangoing but he's behind me. I can feel his cock pressing against me as he follows my prissy legs movement Spade laughs behind him. We're glad Phil ain't here. Arm around waist he thinks about arm around my breasts but doesn't we move on into the blackness the sodium blackness and the sky has been punched out orange orange glowing a garage someone out for Rizlas and fags laughter a car we move to the side now shops with glassed windows and balti houses spilling out revellers with breath like blocked cisterns and there is Phil standing smoking looking round him like a fucking weasel his ringlets bob up and down. He's so fucking prissy before he sees us Danny backs away takes away his warming hot glowing arm from my waist. Phil ain't seen us my feet stop dancing my feet become like bits of chucked concrete I almost want to back away, move into reverse motion and leave before my presence becomes real to him. Two guys leave the balti house. One is cocksure, a leather jacket white man. Big white man. He says something to Phil. Phil looks shocked, startled, shifted out of orbit, and backs away for a minute, his feet dancing, moving delicately arching like a foot-bound girl. But the man pulls at Phil's white shirt at the point where the buttons begin, pulls it away from Phil who moves backwards. Tension between them finds release through the shirt. A loud rip. Phil is cowardly, trying to back down, trying to look subservient like a dog, the glare of his eyes hooded, the whine of his mouth prominent like a sculptured freeze. Where is his bluff sanctimonious fucking exterior now, that fucking face he shoves at me with bravado and self-fucking-justification? I'd like to spit on him. Cover him in my disgust. Just as he did to me when he raped me and spat all over my body, his spit falling on my belly and thighs and breasts, a mockery of coming. Spade runs forward and says, "Hey hey what's the problem? Come on!" Phil's hands are up but the guy has decided he hates his poncy face and punches out at him his mate tries to grab him but an effluence of words he unleashes and his mate backs away he swings at Phil I propel myself forward – why the fuck do I do that? Suddenly I feel hot in the freezing after midnight morning. Danny clenches my side with his hands like pliers, pulls me back says, "Don't," quietly but with profundity but I don't trust the look I see on his face. I could burn under the force of his excitement. Phil's brown hairless chest is exposed and the guy begins to hit him. The first punch shocks me with its strength, and I stop myself from screaming out. Spade rushes forward again but Danny stops him. The guy's mate has stepped back into the shadows. It's just Phil and this leather white guy. The leather guy is winning. A second punch finds his left cheek and Phil sways backwards, falls against the wall with a great crack. I am fascinated as I see Phil's body crash against the wall, his head force down an already ripped poster of an elephant hovering over the tears of a clown's face, his make up seemingly smudged by the rip, his mouth contorted into a smirk, advertising Cottle's Circus from three months back. A slight vengeance of blood runs down Phil's cheek, spoiling the sharp contours of his beauty. The leather man – jacket off, his body twisted into a S shape – muscle tone breaking through his skimpy white transparent t shirt – bends down to Phil, up thrusts his fists two fists so fast they're blurring Phil's legs convulse splay out like a cripple – Danny crushes my belly with his hands, pulls me further away to the side of the shop into a darkened alley, and holding me close to him – Phil's face lopsided, nose a bloody mess – lifts up my skirt – Phil's arms spread away from him – yanks down my knickers – Phil's lips droop open – Danny shoves his cock into me – I watch Phil I peer from the side my head peeking round the wall I just see fists feel violence inside me – Danny fucks me we're standing there I judder up and down but static inside myself – Phil's almost naked shirt torn and hanging from him I imagine them turning him over and raping him – Danny's watching him too – Phil is kicked leather man fed up with the inefficacy or the boredom of using his fists. He stomps on Phil's legs and I'm smiling – I hear them crack – he kicks out again aiming for his chest a hairless beetle's chest easily ruptured – I'm smiling horrified coming smiling

Delaney Wears A Hat

With a hat it's different. They look at me different. I walk into the space and they stare, glare, sneak peeks out the corner of their eyes while pretending not to have seen me. I am here, I am there, I am a clown, buffoon, I exist. I have form and shape of desire. Hatless my individuality vanishes into ether. I exist no more. A face among others existing invisible. Delaney wears a hat.

I know I am hiding. I can see the sky from here. There's a grey and black bird hovering, like a mascot, overhead.

I can see bricks and pigeons squatting, clucking, tides of tension, me looking outward. Towards the blue, the blur of dead-headed shapes, the threshold of blue. Will people notice me missing? Me hiding? Me watching here? Anyone care?

I slip on a hat. Instant visibility and the shapes sharpen. Hat and focus in tandem. The bird is blown out of shape. It lifts, squawks, makes shapes like folded paper.

I come back when it's dark.

Different smell then, different air, different light making halos round the shapes' heads. It's easier to hide. The brimming passing strangers, the wide mouth gape of dour death, the frowning grimacing anal-fisted walks of the dowdy. Sometimes a smell from the restaurant, drifting itching ridging round bricks sidling past fat-bummed polka dot pigeons.

The encrusted dirt-ridden metallic ping of bins, the drift of inhabitation, a smell, the cilia attacked, grimy like green and khaki mixed. That deeply green smell, a scent of underneath, green scum under rings of metal bath taps, the blackened crusty soot of grease from too often cooked unclean oven tops. The smell of forgotten.

I will stay.

Manon said she'd come back, back if they come I am always surprised, gone for an hour, the hour lengthens, in the hour the head emerges, blond, crinkle hair as tight as a hat, curls, a hat, the blond. Then a smile. A smile of beatific. She says don't lurk, don't hide, come out and let me see you. Manon said her smile will save me. She wants to make it all right.

I sit tight. I examine the ridges in the bricks, the ups and downs of the square the square ringing round squares, the rustle and riff of uneven patterning

There's bodies here and bodies there. The smell of something half-rotten, flecks of fur, red and brown and white, black feathers scattered like litter. A stain of blood. And the grey and black escort of crow.

In these ledges, African violets peeking from a soil of scum. I ask is this a hallucination? Those purple heads, the darkening leaves, not green like true leaves, blatant green, ruddy, but blackly purple, like smudged blood licking tongues, as wide as welcoming. Hopeful heads catching stretches of sun, sun particles like ellipsis lines scratching the rusted bitten bricks.

Afterwards, after it has happened, happened inside, an invasion, an alien swallowing, a forcing, what difference does it make? Walking down the street afterwards I am unaltered. My hair is brown, not blue, the sky is still blue and the bees still black and the darkness still heavy. The act, for it is an act, a charade even, showstomping performance, two (maybe more), in roles ill-defined for their bodies, has changed nothing. There is no pre-look and after-look, no signs, signifiers, signposts for the revelation of fucking. So I ask, here in my corner, I ask, here surrounded by metallic bins, hearing noises from the club, seeing shadows on the blue horizon, I ask what does it achieve? Sometimes I wonder what secrets are hidden in here or are they truly just holders of detritus or do they too tell a story pushed deep buried well?

The voices come at me like gusts of wind, voices round corners shouting my name laughing, shouting. Sometimes they stand in the lane, hands on hips and all I see are whites of eyes and whites of teeth and the red of open vulgar mouths. Like slabs of talking meat, speaking vessels.

I don't see why I need move, shift, put foot over edge, put edge into view, put view into sphere of attack. Are their voices going to lure me out, voices like hands grappling my hesitant hidden form? One foot leaves like a soldier AWOL.

The purple of the African violets are drooping, some petals are falling. I catch them, then let them slip, drift, melt between my fingers. I watch little black ants scurry across the fading purple, purple as luminous as deep southern evening skies. I want to crumple the petals' simplicity, tear them apart, make them in pieces, make them small insignificant, cream fading into purple, strips of pieces, strips of what had been whole, feel them tear between my fingers. But I kick my foot out instead, clanging against metal, a diatonic row, a change in metal. The sound scrapes against my ears. I cannot go outside. If I leave I will hate me, hate me in prone position, hate me sitting legs akimbo, hate me crawling arse-tilted. Sometimes I think I will kill them.

They whistle like children, mouths pursed, lips dry but wetting, scraped by pursing, shaped into harsh sounds like tubes, permanently hopeful. Judging. But I won't go, I won't move I won't degrade myself to be like them. Do they think I am so ordinary as to be as base as they? I'll stay here. I'll wear my hat, I'll remove my hat. With a hat I am different. I'll speak slowly quietly so no one can hear me, I'll sidestep into a shape of a ball, arms like swan wings covering my head, or cat's paws licking and smoothing, crawl down, bend over make submissive. (That point when he enters, he any he, all hes, am I in control, am I letting him into me, or am I forced, submissive to my desires?) If he shivers I will rip him to shreds. To submit, yield, capitulate, surrender to what? Desires, will of another, hostage to need and compulsion?

The purple of the African violets are drooping and the lights are coming on in the street – that square of space that's my view – or is it the moon descending like a transparent glove? In the distance I see white tips, slips of paleness and blue and the sound of whispering and plays of sounds, water on sand. I see the ocean, the sea, the drift of water bobbing against the horizon. The blue flows in and out and my head is pulled backwards and forward with the gravity pull. I press on the metal bins, grease grips the slats of the back of my fingers but I won't go. There's kisses on lips and sticky fingers of touch and I think do they know how crazy it all is, saliva, wet, slobbering, dogs after food, and more wetness and then what, you kiss and what have I satisfied? What holes are we full of that a kiss, a fuck and hug will solve? It's just selfish illusion and here I am, they say I should join, jiggle, jaggle my arse, spread my arms in exultation and be open.

I'll rip them to shreds.

The Land is Lighting

We weren't from around there; we'd taken a risk, left the clean, white streets. "Bored," they said, "Let's get out of here. Anyone been...?" No one had.

I'd told them that it was stupid at night; you couldn't see anything once you left the lights behind. And no one knew what it was like out there anymore. It was a risk, I kept telling them. But they wanted to push on. Gissy wanted to push on. "Get there at dawn," she said, "See what it's really like. See what we can find. Or capture." Josh driving. Gissy in the front laughing, playing tapes and lighting Josh's cigarettes, me lolling out on the back seat. A real road movie.

Once we left the city, the darkness surrounded us like an enemy. Gissy said something inane, like "Who put the lights out?" She laughed. Inside the car, in the sudden darkness we felt closer to each other, as if anything could happen and our weaknesses weren't so stupid. So I laughed. Josh laughed. I guessed he thought in the darkness that Gissy's mask would slip and perhaps she would sleep with him. Out there in the darkness, in some desolate field, by a stream, the change of scenery would soften her to him. Alter her.

I knew Josh hadn't thought about Gissy at all. He would consider only the Gissy he contained in his imagination. He had a claim on her I couldn't compete with. Older than me by about three months, he got everything first. He'd been the first to spot her, hanging around our place. He'd been the first to make her laugh with one of his inane jokes. Mad journey, madness leaving the city. I kept telling them "There's nothing out there. It's bare, nothing to do, nothing to see. Why do you think everyone lives in the city?"

In the clean, hygienic cities we live like millionaires, the few poverty areas are our playgrounds, where we go for a little culture, to loosen ourselves. Our home streets are safe, but tiresome, and really mind numbing.

We profit from the poverty here. We trade on its otherness; we visit the clubs, searching out street characters to sell like zoo specimens. Here our people unwind, relax, stains appearing on their shining street clothes. We are explorers, pioneers like in the old West. No more continents to explore: we discover people.

That night we headed southeast even girl-watching had lost its appeal. We could follow the boys and girls round the streets from place to place, lurking in our white automobile, blending in with the gleam of the streets. On the street we looked like pimps and stared like punters.

Every night Gissy's eyes would search out for a particular girl who never appeared. Gissy's resolute face proudly shone under the orange-sodium lights, braving out the stares, the calls, the abuse. Gissy, thin, long arms hanging down her sides like wilted lilies, would move locations in search of this girl, shifting restlessly when she was never found. She never talked about her – nobody really said anything about anything – but I knew the girl had to saturate Gissy's dreams like sweat on a hot summer's day.

Quiet roads heading into the gaining light, creeping up on the dark sky like a girl-stealer, we are heading east, heading south, roads leading straight for the light, gangplanks to God. Behind us, blackness, except for the lights of the city, like a giant wedding cake, layers of light building upwards into the sky. Twenty-four hour lights; the buildings are so tall that the sunlight has to dance between the gaps. Without the hundreds of orange lights, the streets would be nearly black, the day densely grey. The whiteness, the shine of the buildings can't compensate for mere glimpses of sunlight.

We leave our city, our suburbs. Once, years back in my childhood, after the city ate up the countryside, people gradually returned to the glistening concrete streets, leaving the land, leaving their homes for the promise and sparkle of new buildings, new streets, new designs of harmony.

The land is lighting. Now we are able to see the green empty land. Darkness lifting from the ground like fog, retreating like people to the city.

Gissy is quiet, like she's been drugged. Asleep and dreaming. Josh glances at me in the back. Yes, I am still with him. We look at Gissy, her mouth parted slightly, open like an invitation. Josh smiles and turns towards the road.

We can see tumbledown houses, houses in empty fields and everywhere trees, trees, trees. Our eyes are thick with trees, overhanging branches, strangely lit leaves; we drive through trees so dense that it is dark again. The land is reverting to forest. Other patches of ground, near streams, vacant, empty, to no purpose. We turn corners and are confronted by dead houses. Another twist in the road, another house. We feel as if we're travelling through an alien land, or somewhere that has died; but that's obviously wrong, this land is thriving. Gissy wakes and asks. "Where do they grow our food? This is wilderness."

Nothing cultivated. Roses, out of control, in a parody of picturesque, ravaged brickwork, ivy is the new crop, curling, twisting, gripping. Crowds of wild flowers push through what once was lawn.

Josh pulls over suddenly, driving up to a metal gate. "What's going on?" Gissy says, as Josh clambers from the car onto the grass.

"Need a piss." He climbs the gate and disappears. "Coming for an explore?" Gissy asks me. "There's a building over there."

"Sure. That's what I came for." I quickly pull on my boots, but Gissy, impatient, has already gone, heading for the desolate cottage.

Half the walls in front have fallen down and the insides are exposed like an unstitched patient. Gissy wanders around, touching this, examining that; a tourist indifferent to the house. I am more interested in her than in the brickwork, than the shattered wooden floor, the holes in the roof, the remnants of someone's life, soaked, washed out by the sun, left in pieces. I watch Gissy; her face unperturbed, hard and expressionless. I have seen this face out stare guys, backed up in a dimly lit room when the evening got tricky.

I have seen her watch people she fancies. It never changes, only when she laughs. Then she loses her hardness, and ten years, reverts to her girlhood in the suburbs, before they demolished the old city piecemeal and rebuilt it clean and virginal. These were dreams of starting again in a world unmarred by mistakes. There had been no catastrophe in our world, just new visions of cities, like in some rich man's fantasy.

"Don't you think it strange that people lived here? Perhaps were born here..."

"And died here."

"Out here, it's so quiet. They must have been so bored..."

"Who?"

"The people that lived here."

Josh reverses the car and we're heading south-east again. Now the darkness has been eliminated completely. Gissy, after moving to the back, stares out of the window. Josh tells me some tale. But I am watching Gissy, turning round to see what she's doing. If only her face could tell. Josh is indifferent, unnoticing while he drives. But this is Josh completely. He moves on automatic like a machine. Mechanical motion. Nothing contradictory crosses his mind at all, while his hands grip that wheel. Not even Gissy.

The ghostly effect of pre-dawn has vanished under the sunlight and there ahead, the road leading directly to it, a pale sun appears. Enormous, spherical, whole. Unbroken by buildings. It is so huge that I have to shield my eyes.

Josh reaches for his glasses. It is silent in the back. I try to guess what is going through Gissy's mind but she is beyond me; this strange, silent, open-mouthed Gissy, her laughter sloughed away like an ornamental Facade.

Another house ahead. In the light of day the empty landscape isn't so frightening. People live out here, isolated solitary people who cling to the land with the tenacity of the dying. They haven't left for the suburbs, for jobs, for wealth. The silence in the car is unnerving. I want to shout out 'laughter, music, jokes!'

"Josh, pull over here." Gissy opens the door as the car stops and jumps out, shouting, "I like this. I like this." I follow her. The house is much like the last one, perhaps a little more roof, a little more dignity; it hasn't given up yet. Beige brick like huge molars, half-formed rooms. I follow Gissy into the back and find her staring at a heap of belongings in the corner. Something dark red and dingy, a boot torn and ashamed, a Primus stove under a green tarpaulin, a scrap of fabric that was once a red paisley pattern.

Some of the items are so feminine. She touches the plastic and jumps backwards as if expecting to see it move, or for someone huge and wild-eyed to emerge and pierce her to the bone. "Do you think someone's been living here?" she asks, turning to me. Her face is excited, and I wonder if she recognises these pathetic belongings. I stand beside her, honoured, wanting to take her hand. The room is so dark. The walls are like baby waterfalls; streaks of green lichen for wallpaper, peepholes to the outside, plasterboard like bone showing through the green skin. The dampness stultifying.

"The Primus has been used recently," she continues, touching it gently, afraid to feel the rusty metal. We both turn round, hearing footsteps, scrunching through the wood and bricks, and for a moment I feel more than just *with* her; we are partners in adventure.

"I wondered where you'd got to." We relax and Gissy looks back to the pathetic items on the floor. "You know something," Josh says looking around the room, "I'm starving, did anyone bring food?" Gissy squats closer to the tarpaulin, lifts it up, but there is nothing of interest underneath and she moves silently from the room. We follow her out. Josh sits in the other room, open to the sun, and like a cat picks the best position where the sunbeams are most concentrated. He pats his pockets looking for cigarettes but hasn't brought them with him from the car.

Behind the house is a field. Green with stalks of unripened corn. Cultivated. At the brow of the hill I see Gissy, just about to disappear from sight.

"Wait!"

Her tracks across the corn are brief, like a breeze has lifted her and blown her through so that only her toes touched the crop. I follow, heavier than her, my footsteps marking my progress with a crude stamp.

In the valley a house; a real house. Full roof, tended garden. A stream to one side. And no Gissy. I almost expect to see smoke rising from the chimney. I wander around the side of the house, sometimes calling her name. Then I see figures over by the stream – Gissy and a man. The water is free and energetic, it hurries toward some hidden end, and its noise drowns out their words.

I walk towards them, and as I get closer she turns and takes my hand as if bringing me in, as if in need of protection and security. "He lives here, this man *lives* here." I presume he is the grower of crops. He is tall and bony, bearded, hands filthy, as if he had germinated in the earth himself. He says nothing. He doesn't meet my eyes. I smile at him. Gissy is almost dancing. "I didn't believe anyone still lived here. Are you on your own?"

"Some of us are here because there's nowhere else to go." He points to the house. "My family live there but roundabout others live alone." I expected rounded 'r's' in his accent, but his voice is neutral. He is wary like a fox, now staring at us, at Gissy, almost as if he wants to touch, but he backs away if she comes too close. She is excitable, plucking at the thread in her jeans.

"Could we bother you for some food?"

He looks at her and then away, not meeting her gaze. I can sense he is wondering why we didn't bring anything with us. There, in his slight smile, he has taken us for idiots.

"I would love to see your house, talk to you about what it's like to live here. I mean everyone lives near the city, why have you stayed. What do you do in all this space? Aren't you frightened? Also, I wonder have there been any other strangers round here? A girl perhaps, small, thin? This is such a strange way of life. Perhaps I could talk to your wife." The words come tumbling out of Gissy's mouth without pause for breath.

Suddenly he takes flight, rushing off towards the cottage, muttering, "It's best not. It's best not." He has disappeared too quickly for us to believe it.

We feel stranded; out here in the open with just the noise from the stream for company. Gissy laughs and moves off, out towards the trees that follow the course of the water. I walk behind her, thinking about Josh.

"We have to get some food." Suddenly I wonder if we have enough petrol to get back to the city.

"I know. The man said there were others who lived this way. They might be more hospitable."

We laugh; this seems unlikely. Now we are in the trees, giant conifers that stare down on us like sentinels, the ground crunches beneath our feet – dropped cones, bare twigs. "Come on, let's hurry through here." We start to run, Gissy laughing again. She feels no fear. "Don't you think it's odd?" she asks, "It's so quiet here. No music, no machinery, no sounds of people talking and living. Quiet." The trees soon finish and we are in open country once more. To the right a jutting hill, small like a child's outpost, just made for lying on, basking in the sun and watching the surrounding land like a sentry.

We sit on it, not saying anything; Gissy hugs her knees to her chest. I would like to lie flat on the ground but I feel inhibited by her so I sit up and look around.

The land is green and exuberant; I feel over-powered by its strength, the way it attacks my senses with greenness, with its reclamation of a once tamed landscape. I look at Gissy, hesitantly, but she barely knows that I'm there. She is so excited, something has excited her – shining eyes, lips curled upwards, pleased, her fingers can't keep still; they tap against her knees constantly. She looks out, faraway, as if looking at a vision. At home her face is solid, when she laughs there it is not real laughter, not real happiness; I can see that now.

Suddenly she looks down at me. "You can feel it, can't you? It's not just me. I can feel as if something has happened." She is so earnest that I have to agree, and she looks away again, back to her vision. I try to figure out what it is she sees out in this landscape; there are trees, there are hills, there are moors.

For the first time, I want to ask her about the girl on the street. Normally when something happens we accept it; we don't talk about it, as if talking would make it less real. Now I want to hear her say 'She is my sister, she is my friend, she is my lover, she is my enemy, she is me.' But her lips do not move, no answers are forthcoming; I ask myself why

I am afraid. I am still on the streets of Home. I fear these sun-filled spaces; I am only a tourist here.

Way off, we hear shouting.

"Stay here, I'll go look." She nods as I disappear across the heath; she looks comfortable as if nothing will remove her from her seat.

The ground is suddenly chalky and dry, gorse hinders my route. I remember walking, on my way to see Gissy on a dry cold day in winter, through a large crowd gathered to watch a bargain-seller begin his spiel. It was like trying to push the sea-tide backwards, or trying to stop the rain falling with your hands. They had me trapped – I'd pushed so far forward I had the same difficulty which ever way I moved – so I simply gave up and watched them selling tacky china and bedsheets.

Here I couldn't give up. I hear the noises again, this time in a different direction. And dogs, I can hear dogs. I try to climb the gorse, pulling off vibrant yellow buds as I do, but it scratches me like a cat. I shout, "Gissy. Gissy." But I'm drowning beneath the gorse; its branches tear my clothes, graze my face.

To the side a gunshot and something in its lonely sound panics me. I go under the gorse and back to Gissy, my hair snagged and tangled, my face covered with bright lines of blood.

There is no sign of her, no sight nor sound of her. She was never here; the outpost is desolate. I wait. I panic; afraid to call her name. She has gone. She has stood up, maybe dusted down her clothes and taken her leave of me. I feel her leaving for it is a leaving. I feel she has gone. That she isn't just waiting the other side of this gorse. Gissy has gone.

I retrace my steps back through the woods, back past the cottage, stopping briefly to stare inside, to shout inside, to call her name. Nothing, only bare floors and stark walls, no Primus, no frayed fabric. No Josh.

The car is still there. And there is Josh leaning against the bonnet and smoking.

We continue looking until the sun has gone. We continue shouting, searching the bushes for Gissy but we know she has gone. We hang around the decrepit cottage waiting for the owner of the belongings to return. Josh says he heard gunshots but guessed it was just locals. "There has to be more than one." He laughs, lighting up another cigarette. We see no one. Till after dark.

I keep thinking of Gissy. Nothing could stop her from returning if she wanted. By now it is cold, we are inside the car and silent. We are watching the tumbledown house. A shadow appears on the hill, taller than Gissy and not as tall as the man I met earlier. I am sure for no good reason that it is female – the way it walks, the way it talks to the dogs. I want to go out and talk to her, but I am afraid. But I climb out of the car, move towards this nebulous thing. I shout, "Hey! Have you seen..." She is on the hill for a moment and then gone. We think she is the owner of the belongings, and I know that Gissy is with her.

Sometimes we come back to this spot. Josh and I. Though we never leave the car. We just sit and watch the house on the brow of the hill, looking for Gissy. It is a risk leaving the city.

The Sweetest Skin

You could taste the heat, the shrill sounds of children's birthday party, little girls in pink flouncing dresses, fingers as prickly as sticks, such a tease of touch as the butterflies flicker past your skin. Here in the Butterfly House we are lost in the heat. The vividness of the green, the curled shapes of leaves, the tendrils heading upwards, the total absorption of light. And you like a ball of energy, all grasping like static electricity with claws. Bolts of fingers, Adam's Sistine finger and god – you in the halo of light and butterflies like the centre of it, a bursting, smiling radiance.

Everything is planned here. Even your smiles. You know exactly which crease to make, you are conscious of every movement, every breath you take, every syllable you utter, how much air does it take, I wonder, to be you. I admire you; you are the pinnacle of elegance, your outwards persona so perfect. You say, shall we move on? And we float forwards, not hearing the ground crunch, you smiling beatifically at the smudge-faced children, and the butterflies everywhere, every colour, every delicate detail, just reach out hands and touch something beautiful. They flitter like a quick-actioned chameleon tongue. The fragrant petals of flowers are pimps for reproduction, and the butterflies like hapless clients, you tell me. I admire the functionality of such beauty and how everything here moves in useful purpose. Except you, of course.

You're wearing blue. I am in pink. The butterflies fall on you, the blue ones, the Adonis Blues, camouflaged and appearing like water-stains against the shimmering blue. The burgeoning heat from the light hits the glass panes above us and I could vanish in a stream of sweat.

A child says, you have a butterfly on you, and you have, you smile so sweetly. The children swarm round you, all clothed in ribbons and purple bows and bell-ringing shoes and your arms are spread open and the butterflies fall on you like droplets of rainbow rain. And you're so tall and the children like cupids at your feet.

I move backwards, against a tall yellow ochre case, clicking pictures with a cheap shot camera. I turn to look. Crinkled, crumpled half-formed butterfly pupae. They look like a monster's leavings in a nest-like lair, all hanging. I look at you and for a second I see you wrapped up, cocooned, made out of folded filigree wings, hanging dryly, shrivelled like autumn leaves, from a glass ceiling.

The thought isn't unpleasant.

You shoo away the children with the flap of your arms and the butterflies rise like tiny balloons into the air.

You smile at me and we move on. We watch the butterflies supping syrup. I recall you at a gargantuan meal, two rare steaks oozing blood, side salad and a round of crinkly fries, your mouth red with blood and sauce, bit of red-tinged meat stuck in the corners of your teeth as you try to speak, hands gesticulating, knife and fork waving wildly in the air like a mad conductor's baton. You eat well. You collect books, and implements, horde magazines of bygone eras. You have rooms full of books and cases and stuffed otters and foxes' snouts in formaldehyde. You have acres of rooms of paintings. None are expensive. Your wallet doesn't run to the exclusive, merely the indiscriminate and the dusty from cobbled-laned musty shops. The obscure and discarded. You, I suspect, only collect because you don't know what else to do.

You fill up your attics, you fill up your spare rooms that the homeless could inhabit, you fill up everything, you clad your house in pebble-dashing. You are a masked man, you are a hollow man.

I wonder how you'd survive on a desert island.

In a dustless room you look as lost as fungi.

We continue walking. I know why you've brought me here but I don't want to hear you. Your words echo. All I feel is the heat, and the colours. Breath of butterflies dusting me with touch. At the small pond, fountain, a tiny Versailles, we stop and pose for photographs, you smiling sunglasses-clad, me looking a little pale. Then a child, a boy in blue, rushes through, thick and heavy on the bridge boards, and butterflies take suddenly to the sky, jumping in staggered motion, colours in the air. The boy trips, slips, one leg into the pond, the leaves of the lily shake and the flower head breaks. A white flower, coiled and slick, lies lifeless in the bubbling water; its perfection stillborn. We stare at it. You begin to laugh and your voice like a reed, whistling, insubstantial. I want to be able to say something about the waste but you're picking it up out of the water, you're shaking it, you're looking at it, you're flicking it. A blue butterfly, Great Swallowtail, swoops down, landing on your wet hairy arm. The child has made his own way out and is now looking at you and smiling and I want to smack his face. I think if he's so god-like why don't you take him, take him.

I walk away. You're still messing with the flower, wondering no doubt how to preserve it. I've heard you before, you say perfection is transitory, doesn't it make sense to keep it?

I don't want to live in a museum. I wonder if that is truly what you are thinking about us. At first, I thought your collections eccentric and indicative of the eclectic, intelligent man inside, the man these things, – from military history, works referring to the wonders of the world and back to the beauties of the English countryside – truly reflected. How wrong and yet how right I was.

You are a man who inhabits space, you fill up your emptiness in the only way you know how. If you were rich you'd be a Saatchi-style collector but then if you were rich you'd have something about you to make you so. It took me months to understand that these things in your house and your car and your garage and your sheds were in place of thoughts. I tried to engage you about Alexander the Great. You could only point out where items – books, catalogues, dusty prints – lived in your miscellanea. You had everything catalogued to perfection. But you couldn't talk to me about what you knew. At dinner parties, standing in front of illiterate businessmen you could rattle off dates and uniform colours and dimensions of monuments and distances that Alexander had travelled before his young death but you didn't know more that that. You couldn't show me the world inside your head for it was empty. The butterflies are collecting around you.

You're holding court again with the children, but saying nothing. You've taken off your jacket. The children come running, whispered sounds of excitement passing through the bushes and flowers drooping. All colours of children. You unbutton your shirt. The butterflies come quicker now. Landing softly, gathering on your skin as if you are the palest pink flower with a sweet aroma. Wings against wings, jostling like children, children beneath your feet, looking up wanting to touch, arms outright, hands like tentacles reaching up, grabbing onto your trouser leg. You slip backwards into the water. You don't mind, you accept the reverence, the adoration, the brush of wings against your Adam's apple and more come to hail you, the sweetest skin, perhaps you are brushed with sugar solution, are their proboscises tickling you? The children are laughing and adults from the other side of the butterfly house now come to look. Butterflies on your head, shimmering red, black blue, wings like owls, wings like bats, wings like moonstones, covering you, smothering you, wings in your mouth, can you taste their dust, can you taste the tips of their sugar suckers? The children are still giggling but right-minded parents come to take them away and then even more now the butterflies have you. Some children don't go, their parents do. You are adored by foot soldiers. You try to brush them off and some do take to the air only to return but you are entranced. They love you, they want you. You swallow the jewels of them.

When the dust covering begins, when the wrapping process starts, I leave. I take the children too for fear of them getting wrapped in with you. You say nothing. You see nothing. Red-winged Lustrous in your mouth, Great Mormon on your eyes like pennies for the Styx ferryman. I stand by the entrance door and watch you transforming, your skin hazy and golden where the wings don't cover, for once becoming solid and substantial within.

I turn away and a child begins to cry.

Memory of Sky

Now she says it's the springing, and it happens when the memory of sky is most buried, most distant, most like something that's never been, when it pushes at what should be.

It was an act of defiance. Buried slowly, carefully at darkfall, at winter born, at death's birth. They say she followed her thoughts and desires and vanished beneath.

Buried so deep no one can see it and now in the springing the ground pushed water tumbles from the moor like acrobatics. The water gathers beneath her and she can touch it with her finger damp side, the mould of the autumn's leavings. And the memory of sky is like a story told to keep the heart warm. So deep the memory of sky.

The ground swells, makes her itch, the ground bubbles, the ground growls, full of beetles, the ground floods, forming in dark speckles and then they're gone (a memory of sky).

The water pushes up, she lifts her hands to the ceiling, to the coverings, to the dampness of burial. She lifts her hands, feels herself being pushed.

And yet the memory of sky is so radiant she is blinded in darkness. A memory coruscated in halos. The water bubbles and pushes.

At first she tries to stop it, the springing, she bounces on the ground, not wanting to glimpse light, feel light burning her face, sky descending through holes to trap her, (the sky memory as distant as summer) but when the force becomes too strong she relaxes, drifts, lets nature take her (once she saw a bird in here and pushed it back); it was the time of the springing, thoughts of growing, movement in expanse, an inch of revelation like a reverse striptease.

Loosening of body, a drift of acceptance against the comfort of darkness and the mesmer of light. She lifts, arms open, and the layers break down, upward, head into holes, the loosening of water. The ground bubbles into memory of sky. Water tumbles into the dried scraped waterway. A reunion.

Through a tiny hole, the water springs bubbles tumbles gurgles like a child. And she is sliding, slithering into the outside mask (the memories of sky colliding). The mask locks, solidifies a rictus smile, a calcification of survival. A thin reed of sound. She is out. (The striking of sky).

Bubbles to the waterway, waterway to stream, to brook, brook races off rock, through fords to rivers, the river slow, wind-scurried, reed-filled, bird-heard, past boats and fields and marshes and lost tumble-down houses to vastness of sea widening to the horizon of sky.

A Man of Shapes

My lover visits me. He arrives unexpectedly. I open the front door to him, and he stands a little uncertain, smiling carefully, smelling of the sea and a hot car journey.

He brings me postcards, saffron oil to glisten my skin, a lily, and a large silk scarf, in blue and green, to tie about my body.

We walk into the garden, chatting nervously, never touching; the white cherry blossoms like cotton wool buds remind him of home. He takes my hand, pushes me into the Acer trees. We are hidden. The tree's sloping branches grab me, holding me for him, as he touches my cheek. His mouth smells of fresh apples. If only he didn't plunge through my life like water falling over rocks. I touch his arching brows, his small ears, and delicate mouth.

The green and blue scarf, as he ties it around my bare skin, beautifies me. He bows it tightly at the back. I look exotic. His hands run down the silk as if he is trying to merge fabric with skin. He turns me around, pressing me into the tree, parting the fabric of the tied bow, revealing my behind through the triangular scarf shape. His hands tingle against my flesh. The tree branches bow to the ground as I am pressed against them; leaves on me; brittle twigs scratching.

My lover leaves before the day is over and before his marks on me have faded.

I have appointments in town. I ride the tube thinking of him, of only him. A woman with long blonde hair passes me. I imagine him touching her hair. She stands by the door, her hair touches my shoulder. The aroma of fresh green apples. She slips something into my hand and looks at me. I could follow her.

*

Emily smiles. In her living room Emily is smiling. I know she is. Emily always smiles. The door is knocked and Emily kicks off her shoes and runs to it. As she runs, a thread from her cropped grey top catches against in a splinter in the door. I know this is what she does; I have seen her; I can imagine her every gesture.

Emily kisses her lover, though they aren't yet. The kiss catches the girl by surprise. But she likes it. Emily has been known to hand out her address on little bits of paper to strange girls, like me, on the tube. Her new lover is such a girl.

"I bet you have beautiful breasts," she says, leading her to the sofa, where they make love and the new girl leaves before dawn. Emily specializes in girls who have never had a woman before but want to. She can always tell. She can look women in the eye and feel how they want her. This is how she caught me. They talk about their sexual histories, about how they love men but have longed for women too.

Emily washes her breasts in cold water, which makes her feel purged, then she smears white fragrant moisturiser over her breasts and her arms; this comforts her; she fills the house with phantoms and she talks to them as if they are friends come to visit. Sometimes she feels she should never have moved to this crucible of a city.

On the floor she stretches out her right leg a 45-degree angle from her body, and touches her toes, then she pulls her arm over her head, stretching down to her left knee. She counts to ten. She ducks her head to her knees, loving the feeling of stretching along her side and back. She does this daily, almost without thinking, obsessed as she is with her body and its arcs and flow of motion. Her dance teacher says she has beautiful lines.

Emily takes her beautiful lines out into the streets. London is a reservoir of faces to her. Strangers look at her blonde hair, at her litheness, and she gawps like a child at those faces, those bodies. These images she takes back home with her at the end of the day, where she wrestles with their emptiness, and how all her encounters whether corporeal or ethereal, leave her parched. Sometimes Emily feels all those empty people can see right through her and one day they will pick her up and squeeze her essence out through their hands and into the air like helium in a balloon. Emily wishes she could walk above them all, on the roofs of London, picking out those to take home. Like a god, she thinks, like a god.

At the dance studio they are already in action. The men are dancing and their movements and shapes awe her. She never likes to be alone with them. She watches discreetly from the side, looking at them and at herself in the mirror, until they finish, shattered and sweating, and she too can stand before the reflection of her body flexing into perfect shapes. Only then does Emily truly relax.

The men watch her as she limbers up. They watch all the women. Emily thinks that dancing is the most narcissistic profession. Sometimes it makes her afraid and sometimes she glows from the sheer physicality of it. While she is dancing, creating shapes and expressions with her body, Emily doesn't contemplate the phantoms at home, the enormity of the city that somehow she tries to fill with her dreams. Or is that her loneliness she tries to fill with the phantoms of the city? Either way, Emily carries her small-town rebellion into the fat city bursting with women to fuck, and tries to make it mean something. She searches for meaning in the faces of women.

*

The next evening, I visit her again, after seeing her getting off at Golders Green, but this time I bring with me my lover. I should wrap him up like a gift to Emily, for Emily's pleasure, and for his.

*

The man smells of the sea, of cotton wool blossoms and packet travel tissues picked up from motorway service stations. Emily runs away from the unexpected man and woman, towards the window. The back window overlooks an empty garden and a bus stop out on the road. She touches her hands, scratches at them, which she hasn't done so often since a child. It's not that she hates men, she tells herself; she finds them attractive; she finds them funny and exciting. Once she used to sleep with them. But this: this is different, this is an invasion.

The man has a lightness of eyes, a gentle lifting of expression; he could even be said to float through the air as if unhindered by gravity. His pencil thin fingers agitate at his jacket collar. The blue and green silk material pokes out of his pocket. His fingers pick at the material constantly, as if irritated by it. He holds his hands, when away from his pockets, in a curved shape. She could see them being carved by Donatello; how exquisite they look lying together, bent and tucked, like prostrate dancers, or spooning lovers. The man's teeth rest gently on his lip as he smiles. The shape of his smile is almost a parallelogram.

Emily looks from the girl back to the man, wondering if she could have picked on the wrong girl on the train. Normally their sly glances, disbelieving they could actually be seeing a woman they are truly sexually excited by, give them away. Emily plays on this. She practises being small and extremely pleasant and cute. She couldn't have picked wrong, she thinks. Her eye is unerring. The scarf leaps from his pocket with a flourish. Emily had never before made a mistake.

The girl had been good the other day, she thinks, and sweet; she had parted nicely, she seemed used to being told what to do. But, but... this? This is a challenge to Emily. She thinks that it has been a long time since she went with a man. The man is thin and bony and completely unlike a dancer; perhaps she can trust him. She thinks she can cope with what is about to happen. She hopes she is strong enough to experiment as much as she imagines she can. Emily consents.

He seduces her slowly. He persuades her with soft words to loosen her clothes, to show her body, to spread out before him. She takes pride in his gaze on her. His lips taste her hair; he takes pleasure in the textures and the feel of it in his mouth. He is a man of shapes. Her face is fresh oval; under the silk, wrapped about her body, her flesh appears: her arms trapezoid, her bum almost spherical. He likes wrapping Emily in scarves, round and round her, he traverses her contours, creating more shapes, fleshy shapes showing through, little triangle of pubis, rectangles of thigh, hexagon of belly, pentagon of breast, rhombus of back. He touches each shape, following the contour. Emily is smiling; the silk feels fresh and cooling on her skin.

He licks his fingers and invites me to kiss Emily on each available patch; the moist touch of my lips makes her moan. Her flesh is firm. I like watching him take pleasure in such a tantalizing girl. She is so full of life. He says to her, "Beautiful Emily, just beautiful." Then Emily struggles a little and cries out as I hold her down, as my man of shapes fucks her.

*

He vanishes again; I return to the suburbs, barely thinking of Emily and her small flat in the centre of town, with her sublime Beardsley prints, her plump cushions, her dance shoes stuffed like toys into every space. She seemed fine when we left. I kissed her cheek. He kissed her hand. I thought, as she sat there on her sofa, that she looked sexually high. I promised that we would see her again.

But I read about her the next week in the local newspaper.

*

Later my lover visits once more; it has to be the last I see of him, even though I cannot bear my life without him. I let him in; I let him touch me and I would be a liar to say his every touch wasn't a thrill. We make love in the garden again, though the blossom has gone and the trees look overripe. We pick the largest tree. He places me carefully against it. Bark rubs against my arms. I can hear the distant hum of machinery. I am quickly unclothed.

He bends his head to me and the aroma of green apples from his hair reminds me of Emily, I say, "Emily, the dance student, you remember her? The girl I took you to? She died." His tongue is still sticking crudely out of his mouth as he stops to look up at me, as if everything hasn't just changed. "After we left her that evening. They think she ran out into the road into the front of a car on purpose." He looks startled and pulls away from me. I want him inside me and yet am glad he is affected. I wasn't sure he would be. I will miss his mouth, his shapes, making love with him. "They say she made a beautiful shape on the tarmac."

My lover returns to the sea, to gritty sand and to creating patterns with strangers. The white blossoms emerge as usual the following year. I keep all the scarves buried in the earth beneath a white cherry tree. I travel the tube less and never catch anyone's eye.

Vanitas

Time past and time future
What might have been and what has been
Point to one end, which is always present.
T.S Eliot: The Four Quartets

Scene 1: The house
Set back from the road, in a southeast London suburb, with a long bricked front drive, the house seems to have eyes. Behind is the park and a small rectangular passage of wild country, full of brambles and dog shit, that separates it from the next street. Lindy's road abuts it at a right angle. Through the trees from her flat window she can see the house. It seems uniquely separate from the environment. Nothing ever moves there; no bird alights on its immaculate roof; rain appears to bounce lightly upon it before dissipating onto other surfaces; leaves drop away from it; even the planes criss-crossing the London skies avoid casting shadows over the house. She thinks this rather miraculous.

Scene 2: Cartoons
Lindy sitting in her office looks up from her pad, where she is scrawling ideas for her next cartoon. The sky over St Pauls is red like the colour of shame over a woman's body. She puts aside the one sheet of paper that contains images of a thin woman wearing pearls and kitten heels and takes up a fresh sheet of paper. The lead scrawl soon becomes

recognizable as images inspired by Japanese *hentai* and *manga* cartoons. In quick movements, almost as if seeping from the flesh of the hand itself, a child-like woman emerges from the graphite, her facial expression quizzical, a nose puckered in black and white, and her black hair tied in bunches like two fat moustaches on the side of her head.

Behind Lindy, a pale blonde woman walks across the office; others are busy with work, creating a low buzz that fights with the stop/start sounds of the street coming up through the open windows. Now Lindy draws the girl's legs. Opened legs, and a strange hand resting on her thigh. This is what Lindy prefers drawing.

She collects erotic drawings; prints by Beardsley being her favourite; she owns a rare copy of one of his more extreme phallic images. It makes her both excited and amused to look at it, and have it hanging in her living room. Hogarth she admires for his biting wit. Wit in pencil. And for his devotion to life.

While it's impossible to make a living at this yet, the drawing fires her soul as well as partially satisfying her libido.

Lindy lives alone with two orphaned gerbils and a picture of an elephant she sponsors in Africa. And sometimes manages to visit a 'friend' whenever she shifts herself from her living room.

In the next box she draws a male hand – puckered hair, raw bruised knuckles and wrinkles – pulling the girl's clit into an abnormal length away from her body. Lindy laughs and suddenly realizes she's at the office and not alone at home. Clamps a hand on her mouth like a censor, covering up her images with her other hand.

Sometimes she finds it amusing to draw an approximation of herself inside these thick cartoon boxes – thin, boyish, pert tiny tits, strangely long prehensile feet, making sure to show the large wine-stain, shaped like a potato, on her lower back. In these boxes she places herself in clichéd submissive roles: on her knees, looking up to a man or walking slowly across a luxurious room, being gazed at by a man in uniform; domination, brutality and playfulness in contrasting juxtaposition.

Lindy is also a woman of strong opinions who hates anyone patronising her.

She returns to her trendy housewife cartoon drawn for a women's glossy magazine, begins something flippant with egg whisks and fake fur, but in a fit of frustration draws her pallid housewife being shafted by a soldier with a fat dick.

Scene 3: Entrance
The road is full of children playing in the twilight, jumping over skipping ropes, crashing into each other, pulling at hair and shouting. Her tube train pulls away in the distance. The moon is up, hazy and hesitant behind clouds but swollen on the horizon like an eye watching over south London. A slight chill in the air hints at winter. She passes close by the house. At first she thinks the open door is an optical illusion, like the work of Bridget Riley, but the door really is slightly open. Though no sounds come from the interior.

Lindy walks past, looking guiltily towards the door, but the next morning it is open wider, and she looks around to see if anyone else can see what she can see. But others continue on their way. Every day Lindy stares at the house. Sometimes she looks in close up, stopping at the entrance to try and spot movement from a side window, and sometimes she keeps across the road to gain perspective on its enigmatic qualities. Nothing ever moves. No car draws up; no one enters the building with bags of spilling shopping, or leaves close to tears after a row, backing the car away from the house, narrowly running over a passing dog. The house looks lifeless and yet it isn't. She passes the house, feeling it thinking or at least the thought processes of its occupants. It has an occupied air. Busy, hard at work at something important, a palpable sense of purpose. She can almost imagine invisible cogs turning round and round inside, invisibly powered and handled, floating in streamlined pure air.

Most probably the house is a brothel. It must be! But where are its clients?

On the tube, she can't stop thinking of the house, and at work doodles pictures of houses with blanked out windows and secret doors. She wants to know what the house is for, what purpose its occupants put it to use.

Scene 4: The paintings
The painting shows a woman in gold taffeta, holding scales. It is a small painting, but it occupies the whole of one side, and Lindy can barely make out what it is portraying. The light round the painting is focused on the women's hands, spotlighting the smallness. The picture can hardly be bigger than two hands placed together but the woman's expression is clear: it is one of amusement. Lindy reads the text beside it – just as if this were a gallery. It says: Woman weighing her Virtue. Schalcken. On the left hand side the scales contain nothing and on the right hand side heavy jewels. Lindy nods as if in agreement, and feels her stomach bite.

At the other side of the room is a large painting; the image is of a young man holding a skull, his right hand spread out towards the view as if demonstrating a point. *Vanitas*. The text, in bold print, says: *This is a reminder of the transience of life and the certainty of death*. Fran Hals. The two pictures stare at each other; one larger and more domineering, both there in such opposition for a reason. Around Lindy the rest of the walls are bare. The focus of the room is on these two paintings. If she stood in the centre of the room and placed her arms at right angles to her body, outstretching them as if trying to touch the very crackle of the surface of the paint, it would seem the paintings were pressing against her, as if they wanted to press the images of themselves upon her body, like tattoos.

She stares at the paintings till sounds in the distance pull her back to the surface, away from the smell of turpentine.

Scene 5: Authenticity
At first Lindy is hesitant to enter but the house is open for a reason, and her curiosity forces her through the door. The acrid smell of burnt lemon, mould and turpentine hits her immediately and she just stops herself from gagging by holding her hand across her mouth.

She moves upstairs, following a small androgynous figure that had appeared suddenly from the left. The modern reproductions of Victorian-style lamps light the passageway. From its walls, of smooth red William Morris wallpaper decorated with images of peacocks, hang, from a picture rail, famous paintings: bathers humped over a bright blue river by Seurat, and a Paris street at night by Pissaro, Picasso's peace dove and child, and a big-headed *Laughing Cavalier* by Frans Hals. She doesn't know if they are original or just copies. They hang there, solid, beautiful, astonishing with the appearance of authenticity. Lindy stares at them. Some she has seen in museums.

The figure ahead of her moves onto the stairs that angle up the right hand side of the house. She is expected to follow. She passes one open door to the right of her that exudes nothing but dark silence. Music begins, from the left hand corridor – violins slicing through the dusty air. A dog races along here towards her smelling of rain and lemon shampoo. It rushes downstairs and out through the open door to the bright outside, flicking water, as it passes, onto her hands. Cold water.

Then she nearly trips on a fatheaded sunflower taking up the space on the next step. It lies prone like a beheaded blonde darling – all curls and sun-flattered. The music gets louder, violins shouting with cellos for clarity. The sunflower lets loose all of its seeds. They tumble down the red carpet like little black eyes.

Scene 6: House of Fakes
At first the people are daunting. She sits among them trying to look animated. Paper-laden sofas, pale hands casually turning hefty books surfeit with pictures, papers scattered on the floor like rugs, unstable towers of videos, pencils in a multitude of colours lying like mosaics on a veneered table. Someone begins reciting T.S Eliot:

"If all time is eternally present
All time is unredeemable.
What might have been is an abstraction
Remaining a perpetual possibility
Only in a world of speculation.
What might have been and what has been
Point to one end, which is always present.
Footfalls echo in the memory
Down the passage which we did not take
Towards the door we never opened
Into the rose-garden."

In ones or twos people leave the room. Androgynous figures coming in and out of the side door with smiles on their faces. It feels as if they are waiting for something. She feels panic, she feels like a fake coming in here. She has no business here. At one point she stands up but someone gently pushes her back down. Talk, like a highway above her head, buzzes through her ears. She catches the words like one might recognize the flash of a badge belonging to a passing Aston Martin, or TVR. She tries listening harder. Sometimes the words sound like genuine English, other times she thinks she catches Dutch words, or German or Italian, and then sometimes she can recognize nothing. And it is as if their tongues have been possessed by demons.

She gawps at the sounds.
  She gawps at the room.
  She wants to touch every beautiful object.

The room spins like a fairground waltzer.

Scene 7: Extremity
Lindy is alone. The lights are down. Music is playing. The room is wide and cavernous as she has pushed the furniture back against the walls. The floor is littered with cushions. Velvet cushions, silk cushions with lurid tassels. She turns the TV on, sits back against the cushions with pad, a HB pencil, a small lamp. By her side a tapered candle and incense burn. The smell of musk fills the air. Lindy presses 7 for the video channel, grabs the video remote, presses play, and fast-forwards the boring bits. Soon the images she desires fill the screen. She looks around her empty flat in case the walls are watching. She is partly scared. She always feels partly scared. Within five minutes the flabby girl on the screen is caught from behind and in terror, it seems, is forced to open her legs by a large man who quickly becomes naked. More men join the scenario. And soon the woman is smiling. Lindy is appalled at what she sees and her own reaction to it. It is as if she is two people. Her face flushes. She continues watching and makes rapid sketches.

Scene 8: A face of caricature
Then suddenly from the right a hand grabs hers. She is led away from

the chatterers, and through a side door. The hand holding hers feels sticky and warm like it has been sitting between its owner's legs. Still it clings onto her, pulling her from the main room towards corridors and stairs spiralling up into the heart of the house.

Without warning the person halts in front of a door that looks very much like all the other doors. Solid, brown, and shiny. It holds no special significance in terms of shape or size. It has a big green handle the size of a billiard ball, and four panels. On one panel is a long scratch as if an unknown person has deliberately created the gash with a car key. No sounds come from the room beyond. Lindy looks at the figure as he stands away from her, smiling slightly, lips bending to the left-hand side of his face, and wonders if she is dreaming the nervousness she sees there.

He says, "Take your time. Most people find they enjoy the experience but many don't like being confronted." His face is like a thin dog's: nose elongated, eyebrows wide and plump like hairy slugs. And his chin heavy in the middle but thinning as it juts out, ripe for pinching. Or drawing like a Scarfe cartoon. His eyes protrude as if they are mini domes of St Peter's.

"Confronted by what?" she says, entering the room.

He looks at her strangely as if it is obvious that she should know. "Look."

Scene 9: Imaginings and reality
A painting: a house. Mist. Soft lighting. Charcoal lines in sepia. The front of the house is like a mirror; glass; water. Soft footsteps in the distance. A man stands beside her. Tall, well built, long limbed. Then he is behind her. A man curls his arm around her waist, touches her breast. Someone to one side looks at her and then is gone. Bliss in the touch of his hands as it sidles up her skirt touching her carefully on the thigh. She begins to breathe heavily. This is really happening. She likes it and yet feels out of control. The house focuses in on her. Normally her fantasy is of this – a man standing behind her, grabbing her breasts, even down to someone else watching; she loves the image of it.

She sees the Schalcken painting to the right and then the Hals to the left. She sees all the fakes: the people in the living room, the highway of words, the other paintings. She likes this touch on her thigh. This is really happening. He moves aside her knickers, thrusts thick fingers inside. Oh god this is really happening. Fingers touching her. Better than any image: video or drawing. She is coming so fast, it is as if she hasn't been touched for years. But she can't control it, it can't be right, she can't accept this. It's been forced on her. This man is a stranger!

The room spins.

She sees fake paintings. She is out of control: loose-limbed, mind taken elsewhere, breathing getting heavier. She wants to push down on the mauling hands. A stranger's hand. What sort of man, clean, sexy, interesting? The fingers thrust. Part of her wants to respond to him, let him do whatever he can do to her and yet.... She pushes against him, pushing with her cunt muscles. Breath on her neck, he pulls down her top, pushes the bra cups beneath the mound of flesh; her breasts are exposed. She will be seen, she fears the laughter of unknown eyes, but still she is coming. His fingers are wet as they thrust in and out. She pushes against him with everything she is, till separating from his wet strange fingers and runs away.

Scene 10: Bathos
In the passageway she alters her clothes. The door is closed behind her. Piss runs like fear down the inside of her leg coiling out of control as it hits her shoes and the floor, seeping into the carpet. The lemon-scented dog trots past, this time glancing at her as he continues. The androgynous man appears from nowhere, opens a door on the opposite side of the room.

She doesn't want to go in. She fears more confrontation.

"It will be ok now," he says. "It's going to be what you actually prefer."

Scene 11: Safety
The room is of nothing. Silence. No wallpaper, no paintings, no images, no excitement. No music. There are no statues standing on plinths, no touchable objects. Nothing to adore, or adorn. The room is of nothing. It has no perceivable boundaries, no definable barriers to place a warm hand against, but nevertheless it is a box like any other room. Her hearts' desire is empty.

The emptiness scares her.

She grabs the air for comfort.

Hands reach out, claw-like.

She cannot feel a floor nor see a sky nor a painted ceiling. The infinite feel of the box appals her.

In the distance, seeming to hang from nothing, is the image of a painting. The image of a young man holding a skull. Vanitas.

Scene 12: Lines on a page

Lindy at work looks to the skyline. No longer is it shame-red, but a light pastel blue. She thinks the sky has the light the wrong way round. It should always be blush scarlet. Sometimes while working she remembers the house and her cowardice.

She has a deadline but she cannot think. She doodles and in doodling swirls up a *manga* image, which for a second pleases her, but almost in the exact second of pleasure at the created image she immediately transposes it into nothing by the addition of more black lead. So much so she rubs away the surface of the paper, creating an empty hole, exposing the pattern of the table underneath.

Lindy begins drawing again on a separate sheet of clean white paper. She draws a thick box exactly 3 inches by 3 inches on the centre of the page. She draws three boxes in an exact line down the page, one underneath the other. In 3D. Precise and symmetrical but empty, transparent, bereft of everything but thick black lines across the centre of each panel.

Saft

He said he was a saft bugger and the hem of his jacket was frayed as if bleached and teased by the teeth of dogs or pulled through a hedge or through one of them pulley machines you see in museums of old life.

John didn't care about hitting him. The man was there, that was enough. I said if he went near him I'd go but John was adamant. The guy was there, stiff hair, frayed jacket and nose like a funnel on an ocean liner.

I tried to pull him away but you know what he's like when he's got something going, some ridiculous refrain in his head, crazing his head like a Kylie song – the guy's there – he's standing there, in his patch, in his space, where he goes everyday, where people know he'll be, where they expect to find him, by the railing, where the breeze off the river blows just for him in his personal space and where the leaves in autumn lift and circle him like a spiralling halo. He'd been standing there for years.

He's got to be a saft bugger, just standing there. Doesn't he know, he said, it's my space. That's my tarmac, my bench, my effing railings, my white lines on the ground. My fucking air. I pulled him away again. I said, you hit him, I aint coming back.

My space, he said, my space, you can't expect me you know, let him stand in my space? Everyone knows it's mine. Mine. The fucker's mad. He dropped his fag stub on the ground. He's got to be mad.

I said it again but John moved forward towards the guy, the saft head, the crazy fucker, standing there his nose funnelling the river breeze, gripping the railing like kneading bread. Does anyone knead bread anymore, I thought, backing away, trying not to watch John step forward, his legs with big strides, mountainous strides, strides across continents. Arms out, he grabbed the guy's jacket, frayed cuff, frayed collar, he yanked it, the guy toppled forward almost into John's arms just as John reached out up and across with the other hand, like a dance, a patterned shape between them, each responding to each other's motion. They're dancing together, leaning forward, moving backward in a parody of a tango. I turned away as fist chimed with chin, the sound of ringing bells in bone.

John turned towards me but I was gone. He's a fucking safthead, I heard him yell. A fucking looney!

Limbo hours

The box surprised her. It was blue-green. Office colour. And light. She lifted the cardboard lid which fitted so neatly, so perfectly. She admired the sound of it coming apart from its other half. But it was empty. Its shape and form was a crucible for nothing. She walked across from it, leaving it sitting in the centre of the room – it was not what she was expecting: such air, such vacuity of purpose – and just looked at the empty box for some time, till dusk turned to dark and she closed the blinds.

The coffee was hot. She sat holding it. She'd ordered a venti latte and its richness almost made her gag. Starbucks was empty. Nina Simone played to vacant tables and the coffee makers, graduate students mostly, looked restive as if capable of starting a revolution. Then she put the plastic cup on the table and looked through the vast array of glass to the outside but the street was silent for a moment. No traffic turned the corner up the hill, no one walked past down to the centre of town, nobody came up from the station. All she could see were reflections of herself in glass windows. She didn't know why she'd come in here really, except it was what she always did after work. She didn't feel like filling herself with liquid.

She left the coffee half drunk and steaming and walked out into sudden crowds where she was safely subsumed.

The box hardly made a difference to her life. She took the rubbish to the binmen collection point on Thursdays, got up at a normal time, caught the 7.15 to the city, logged on at work, marked her mark in the electronic version of her existence. All was well. These were her outward signs of functioning. The box sat in her living room still. She put objects in it sometimes: a red ribbon, a yellow candle, a book of Chinese poems, an Ansel Adams mountainscape postcard, a steel framed mirror, an elm hairbrush choked with twisted red hair. Then she took them out again, one by one. And left them on the side. Now she forced herself to plan her day in hourly intervals – *at this time I get up, at this time I do the washing, at this time I bathe.* This is structure, she said. This is the way of moving forward.

But instead the house around her felt structureless and transparent, to neighbours or passing strangers; everyone could see her pathetic movements; if the house was see-through then so was her body. She had pellucid skin; she had bones made of glass, organs of crafted Perspex, genes as obvious as rainwater. Even her thoughts from her hollow head were written out on ticker tape and thrown to the eyes in the sky.

She drank gin in the early mornings/late nights by the French window and watched the moths desperate for entrance, and listened for the terrifying howls of suburban foxes that penetrated the very hollowness of her. It was a strange time of existence – neither night nor day. It was the middle of nothing. Limbo hours of breathing. Sometimes she opened the doors and looked out at the in-between sky and, though it was filled with zillions of stars, all she noticed was the enormity of the spaces between them.

The Cusp of Something

We were looking for the face of the Buddha in the limestone rock. We were looking for happiness.

"Stand back," Jiro said, "And look at the rock. If you see the face you are guaranteed happiness." He looked directly at me for the first time in days.

We stared. We stared as if our life depended on it, and made out patterns in the rocks: a woman sneezing, a boy on horseback with a crooked arm, a girl coyly looking up at an unseen viewer. There were some boys standing behind us but we took no notice of them.

"No face, then I guess that's happiness out!" I glanced quickly towards Jiro, who had begun to laugh wildly and cough as if something were stuck in his throat. The boys behind us put their hands to their mouths and moved away, heads down, fearing catching a cold. Without looking at me, Jiro hurried away up the steps. I sighed. This was now monotonous and tiresome.

I must find this face in the rock, "Can anyone see it?" It must be here somewhere if there's some story about it.

We stood. The light shone on us, from between the trees. I was wrapped up warm; too warm really, as it had turned out to be not as cold in the mountains than we had been told, than the snow cloaking the valleys had led us to believe. It was the cusp of spring, the cusp of something, *sukura* trees just budding. I was sweating, gloves stuffed in pockets, spare jumpers wrapped round my waist and hat folded like a fajita into my top pocket.

All around us lay the objects of mourning: old stone tablets, lanterns to light the way, and also objects of prayers for good fortune: baby dolls for newborns, red knitted hats on small stone Buddhas, plastic garish flowers, Barbie dolls grinning madly, and little rows of red soldiers tumbling over rocks.

Everyone was growing restless, looking at the rockface for this guarantee of happiness. We were an odd collection of pseudo-freaks and suburbanites, always moving, always looking for ways to make time go faster. Randall kicked against the wall, repeating the kick again and again. Funny how much he looked like a yobbo when he put his back into something. The shape of him, heavy and scary. I liked him, he was easy to get on with even though he was a merchant banker, travelling the dirty commute trains to London from the Surrey borders daily, reading the latest thrillers, the latest headline-making books in the *Evening Standard*, which he left, crumpled and used, on the blue striped seats when he reached his station.

He was orderly and strong and looked unencumbered.

He liked strip clubs and sat all night on the internet surfing for the dirtiest porn. Played rugby on wet grey Saturday afternoons. He no longer asked how my other half was, or if my other half wanted go for a pint with him.

I looked away from the rock to the view across the mountains full of shapes, bulges and slanted lines, sweeping lines of trees. Barbs shouted that she thought she had seen it. So we all crowded round her. Everyone but Jiro who was busy pulling a red woolly hat off a Buddha. Maybe he was looking at me, but I couldn't be sure. Nor could I tell how embarrassed he really was or how much of it was my imagination. Perhaps I wanted him to be embarrassed. But he should know by now that I couldn't bear anyone. I'd discussed it with him enough times over sake and in wind-chilled darkness when everyone else had gone to bed.

"Where?" We asked Barbs. "Where is this face?"

Japanese were wandering down the steps looking at us *gai-jin*, not realizing that Jiro was actually with our party. Barbs pointed to a cutting, a space worn away by weather, by time, and someone said but that's a horse!

We laughed and moved on. I kept looking back at the rock, desperately trying to be the one who saw the face. The group moved up the steps; I slotted in behind lovely Gabriella, as she shivered and shoved her hands deep in her pockets as if a sense of death had suddenly touched her delicate cheeks.

The temples from below looked like a series of cable cars climbing up the side of a mountain, red and rising.

In the water, hot hot water, in the sky buzzards and my skin uncovered and sunlight finding me. An open air *onsen*. Bizarre to be here, naked in the open-air, uncomfortable at first, but an excitable feeling of decadence and liberation. I smile madly. It's like an unloosening.

Buzzards howling above. Other women coming in and out, holding up their modesty towels, no one looking at each other. Cold air on reddening skin as I climb out and sit on a rock. Hot steam on my face and body, cold meeting heat. Alone now and relaxed. And free.

Then I slide back down, tingle on the skin, feel the hotness beneath, between my legs and serenity take over my body while feelings of floating, disassociation take over my head. I reach out my arms. Now I am alone in this pool. Water flowing over rocks. Arms floating on steaming volcanic water. Wind through the bushes. The buzzards again, fighting with crows, in the trees over the road. I stand up and peer over the corn-coloured fence. The road is below, and the ravine, and slow groups of people walking, passing traffic.

Suddenly, from over the other corn-coloured fence made brighter in the sun, come the deep guffaws of men's laughter. I try to imagine if the men's onsen is a mirror-image of here and whether Jiro with his sensitive rashy skin is finding it uncomfortable. It's so good to be away from him, away from noise and just be alive.

Gabriella, she of the cheeky smile, the welcoming assuring smile, comes over from the other pool and sits by me. I notice for the first time how sturdy her legs are, how large her thighs. She touches me accidentally. I touch her arm as I stand up. Her skin is soft and aromatic. I could breathe her in. I could just reach out and touch her. She'll be warm to touch. She'll be breathing and warm and surrounded by steam. I could just touch her.

I could stay here forever.

Until my fingers crinkle and I am washed away merging with water.

Outreach arms, spaces in my head and floating away like rivers. Bell-water, water through bamboo, cries in the sky, the squeal of bubbles, whispers through bushes.

I try not to think about having sex in the water. I try not to think about it, as much as I want it. Nor do I think about the man who had left me.

We peered over wooden poles to look at innards of temples. We tinkled with bells and fingered paper twisted hangers. We looked and stared and bought good luck charms and rosary beads to wear as ornamentation around our wrists never for praying, we hung our heads over the display and picked out blue and pink hangers in embroidered wrappers for the car. "Don't look inside," Jiro said, explaining he had opened his once when he was seven. I said, "That's typical." Jiro stared, such a cold expression, such stillness, a mask of dispassion. He was never going to forgive me for turning him down, for being 'remote' as he called me, for being cold and a tease and someone who shamed him with denial. He didn't understand. He thought everyone was like him, a beach bum from Brighton, into aromatherapy and freethinking, punky haircuts and a perennial tan. I must have been mad to come with them all. We had so little truly in common anymore.

We panted our way to the top. I thought about hermits living in the small caves or monks praying in temples, about the depth of winter here and everything burdened by snow, and I wondered if I should pray silently to myself, mumble words through my fingers, wonder aloud to Buddha, to good luck charms in plastic bags. "Find something," Gabriella had said, "To replace what you have lost, what is no longer yours. You have to find something." I knew this. I knew about the hollowness inside but could it be replaced by another man?

"Basho came here," said Jiro and he began reciting. "*Shizukasa ya / iwa ni shimi-iru / semi no koe*. Shall I translate? Silence! / penetrating rock – / the voice of cicadas."

I nodded. I took pictures. Everyone took pictures. We congregated on a platform overlooking the distant mountains. The valley looked idyllic, like a Swiss scene, red pointed roofs and a flat straight road. The breeze chilled my cheeks, though I was steaming beneath my moon coat. A small Japanese woman, in a beige padded jacket and Burberry scarf knotted round her ageing neck, shoved a camera and smiled politely in front of my face and pointed to a smiling family standing by the parapet. I nodded and she rushed back to them. I took the shot. They smiled. Another shot. A cloud, resembling a humpbacked whale, slotted into view, all wispy and bulging and luminescent as the sun caught its shape.

Young and old stood with their hands wafting in the incense bowls. Good for brains, they said, breathing in the heavy jasmine scent, the scent of jasmine soaking into our heads. After a group photo, taken by me, everyone split up again, moving about the temple floor. Jiro ran off, away into the trees, climbing above the temple. I took pictures of reddened bark in sunlight and buds forming. "Bailey," Randall turned to me, pulling roughly on my coat, "It says this is where some geezer," he stumbled over the name, "buried a manuscript of a Basho poem here." The ground was covered by a mouldy bronze plaque. "What's good about this place?" he said.

For Randall, the pure air, the delight in watching the flow of mountain ridges across the horizon, to trace patterns in rocks and colours of cusping trees rolling down the back of hills, couldn't do anything for him. The air was so crisp it could freeze lips.

"Is this just a bunch of old buildings to you then? Don't you feel anything else?"

He laughed and shrugged and walked away, shouting, "I can't help it if I'm just a pig! Where's my motorcycle!" he yelled, imitating revving up his Moto Guzzi. "A fast car! A bevy of sexy girls!"

We walked higher, up to the next level, the next esplanade of wooden temples with sloping roofs and wafting incense. Jiro had vanished. It was very quiet, very civilized. People going past so quietly, the air chilly, my skin hot from exertion, not knowing which direction to go in. In the stillness I waited to feel, for something to touch me; I outstretched my arms, waiting. The breeze. Trees budding, while at their feet drifts of snow. Waiting. This is the very cusp of …?

At the top of the monastery we climbed a cliff. On a chain. All of us in a row, Randall first, to hold the chain at the top. Barbs was scared. Little

Barbs with her flick-back hair and piercing blue eyes. She hesitated and her bag drifted off her shoulder. "Do we have to go up here?" She embarrassed me, stupid girl, I thought. I was just glad it wasn't me. I pulled on the chain, lifted myself up, pulled myself to the top on strong legs. "Bailey! Wait for me," she shouted, "Don't go without me," as if I was her guardian. She was small and delicate and doll-like, so men thought, wearing a coy expression when anyone spoke to her. No one would think she was a forty year old woman in a high-powered management job.

"You're strong enough," I said. "Think of the rope as an oar pushing through the water. You can do it."

"It's not the Thames," she said, "I don't want to fall backwards."

All the men were now at the top, even Jiro who had come running from somewhere. Up here in some secret place. We were high above the other tourists and Jiro was smiling. That made me nervous.

They'd gathered like parrots huddled in vibrant colours. All the men, black hair, brown hair, hair with glints of red. I clambered over the top, scuffed my jeans on the gravel. Jiro helped me, but I shook off his arm. Touch was like a promise. I didn't make them anymore. The residue after the end of a relationship was never pleasant, the way it left you feeling as if the world had become unstable, leaving you feeling nothing but hollow and insecure inside. As if all the certainty in the world had vanished like twists of smoke into a grey sky. You'd think Jiro would know this. He thought I could now just attach myself to him as if none of that mattered.

I wondered what the others here were seeking to replace? Barbs, a lost baby, an inability to conceive again, Randall, the fact his career had stalled. Jiro, no one wanted to lay him, and Gabriella? I looked at her climbing the chain, trying to imagine what she could lack. She had a lover, she had a mother and pets and children. Sometimes she looked at me strangely. She lived on the Thames opposite Eel Island in a salubrious apartment and sang to herself when she thought no one could hear her.

Grace and certitude.

We all lacked something.

They never asked about my newly-emptied home, or why I showed so little interest in them. No one asked any questions. They only wanted to hear good things. Did that mean we were no longer truly friends? They seemed to want to run away from everything else. All they were doing was looking for the next thrill. I could understand that.

Waft incense into your brain, baby, helps with the mind, pray at temples, wear beads round your wrist, take hope and succour from whatever offers it. Gabriella at home often treated herself to Indian head massage and reiki healing. She even meditated and listened to the words of the guru. But it seemed to me she really thought of no one but herself. I said to no one in particular, "Is Buddhism the selfish religion?"

The face of the Buddha was self-contained. It needed no one to reflect its glories, it needed no one for approbation. Look how still the face was. Look how perfect, serene, looking inward. It saw not the hawk around his head, the hawk diving and bombing, circling. The hawk was alive. The heart beat, pulsed, raced. The hawk lived. The face of the Buddha was made of stone.

The mountains were so touchable. Like folds in the body.

"Now all we have to do is walk back down again," Randall said. Everyone groaned. The sun was in our eyes.

1100 steps.

Too many steps.

The man comes in now and the nervous chattering in the room stops as he bows gently and places little trays and lacquered containers of food on our tables. This takes a long time. There's lots of food. Waves of trays, waves of polite young men and women it seems with gentle smiles and delicate bows. He points out what the food is and Jiro translates: miso soup, tofu and some weird looking sauce, some jelly-like stuff which I place into my mouth and immediately want to gag. It has the texture of those jelly shoes that kids wear in the summer, all chewy, rubbery and shiny.

"*Konnyaku,*" says Jiro, "from potatoes." The fish wears an appearance of horror – mouth wide open as if about to scream. It's lying there small and crinkled, a river-fish whose name I can't comprehend. The names are befuddling and I don't ask Jiro to repeat it. But the fish is looking at me, it's not flat on the plate, but upturned in motion as if just lifted from the river and embalmed for eating.

I tear into its white flesh, ignoring the evil eye.

"Raw venison," they ask. Why not? It comes round and shaped like a rose in a whirl. There's a sauce too. I open another little lacquer box and there's something else. Vegetables shaped like emblems, string bleached white stuff that crunches. Then there's rice. Lots and lots of rice in a beautiful bowl. I struggle with the chopsticks. Everyone but Jiro struggles with the chopsticks though Barbs is getting the hang of it. It feels like a feast of Caligulan proportions. More food comes through the door. Little bowls of sake in red. We all *Kampai*. The food is texture food, delicate tastes, this merging with that, place the tofu in the sauce, he says.

"Is this normal food for Japan?"

"Traditional, yes," he says.

"No meat and two veg, then," says Randall. We laugh while stuffing textures in our mouths. The flavours tingle the taste buds. Not used to such gentle and alien tastes, I feel as if my mouth has been hit by the sweets I ate as kid, Angel Dust. Alive with taste. We are alive with senses on this trip, the sensual covering over god knows what.

I crunch tempura, the batters seeps between my teeth and then I find the vegetable hidden inside.

"I understand why the Japanese are thin," I say. "This isn't exactly comfort food."

"You need comfort food? Don't you like this? That's pathetic."

We look a little sheepish, every one of us. "It's different."

"It's an experience."

"A challenge!"

"None of you can handle chopsticks! You're all Neanderthals!"

"I like the way the different tastes and textures interact, the different flavours in my mouth combined with the sauce. It's an experience dipping one thing into something else."

"Do they have seaweed with everything?" asks Gabriella.

The fruit is easy to eat. Delicious sweet small strawberries and kiwi fruit. I suck the strawberry into my mouth relishing the sweetness. Jiro watches me. His mouth slightly open.

His arms are on me as I reach my door. He fumbles roughly. Tries to touch my face. "You want me," he says. "I can feel it."

I push him away; try to get the key in the lock. "You've drunk too much *sake*." He's back again, now pulling me round to him, grabs my breasts. I won't scream. "You're too full of everything," I say, "You're drunk." I push him off. But he tries to stop me moving.

"Maybe," he says, "But you wanted me once. At least I thought you did."

"Everything's changed, don't you understand? Everything's changed." I can't go from love to sex. I kick his knees then slide the door open as he crumples up in pain.

I lock it behind me. Thank god I am alone, not to have to wear a face and look good, and nod in the right places and care for what others think. The time for caring about the opinion of others has passed.

The futon looks welcoming. I throw off my clothes and get inside and just lie there, listening to the other guests making their way back to their rooms. I think about Jiro and my fingers find their way between my legs. It's comforting there. I drift toward sleep, thinking of Jiro, of his fresh young skin, his wide warm smile, wondering how he would fuck. I imagine him inside me. He's good to use like this. At least he's real and wants me.

I miss the touch of others: arms on my body, flesh on flesh, breath on my neck, and the approbation of a human smile. I try not to think of him. Why should I risk letting anyone in anymore? The breath of humanity on my shoulder, warm, and wonderful, is illusory. It can't be trusted. An initial warm touch masks the inevitability of coldness. Of being alone in mountains of cold breezes, and chilly hands and the desire to fill yourself with anything and everything to replace a lost love. I touch myself. No pain in my touch on myself. It's the only true authentic feeling: the touch of your own finger on your own clit. The only pleasure you can truly rely on.

The monastery behind us, we huddled round a large Toyota people-carrier, eager to find somewhere to eat, to get away from the cold and the wind. "I want those sweet things once more before we fly home," says Gabriella. She really was lovely, I thought, standing near her, taking in her warmth. Jiro stood on the opposite side of her. There was something wholesome about her, despite her ultimate selfishness. Jiro smiled up at her, touched her hand, and whispered, "The coffee place here will make you delicious ice-cream and fruit, like none you have tasted before. As sweet and as succulent..." and I felt like throttling him.

The *sukura* trees were budding, and we had killed time with tastes and textures in our mouths, watery heat on skin, dropped through air and space, seen wooden buildings with decorations and incense. The mountains formed an inflexible crucible. The wind grew stronger and our car drove away.

I watch Jiro as he leaps from the cliff and spreads his arms out. And then Barbs, and Gabriella. Look at them all flying like hawks. I'm hesitant, maybe a little scared. But I am always scared. Me and Gabriella love this, though she's never as scared as me. She just jumps. She loves floating. It's the biggest kick – out there in the sky. She does it every weekend she can. Mountains are launch pads for freedom. The monastery is behind us and the valley below and we will conquer the air with our shapes. One by one the others jump. I imagine, for a second, their parachutes not opening, the red of the Japanese flag not spreading out across the sky, circles of dying suns in the air. The valley below covered by floaters. How close we all are to non-existence.

Someone is behind me as I teeter on the edge. Vertiginous cliff below. Randall. I touch his fleeced arm. My feet over the edge, pull back. But Randall, heavy, can he really fly? Can the air truly hold him, won't he crash through the blue of the sky? He leaps. I can't believe it – he is held by air. I will join them all soon. I will stretch out my limbs, jump upwards into the air as if it was tangible like a hole, and I will taste wind and my heart crazy-beating in chill air. I am last to go.

It's the only thing left, isn't it, to leap into the air, to leap into nothing, forget the world you leave behind, to do nothing but experience without thinking, and gulp air and live, take in huge fat breaths of air and float to the ground like a crazy leaf.

The Lightest Blue

Three rolls of used film sit on a grubby white bedspread, where they've been for the last six hours, not shifting an inch since my girlfriend Jude left the hotel room. Even though I've dropped clumsily onto the bed a number of times, they haven't moved; they cling tightly to each other in the centre space, like compatriots. I barely contain the urge to hurl them around the room.

Instead I have been amused by crass Greek adverts on the TV while I've emptied my room bar. First Red Bull and Pimms, and now I am liberally drowning in *retsina*, which is revolting. It stinks of mould, of sharp pine, like loo cleaner. While it's liberating being drunk alone, the room feels hurried as if it can't wait to be rid of me and reeks of toiletries – lavender room spray and lemon disinfectant – and Jude's expensive perfume. I haven't eaten since this morning's rolls. The immensity of the space is frightening. Without her the room and the city feel monstrous.

Footsteps in the passage, clinking heels. She has tiny feet. Of course these particular feet walk away past my door and I feel like a stupid for hoping that she has returned, a fool who puts his trust in people.

It occurs to me, suddenly and with frightening certainty, that of course she must have had an accident. What is scary about this is the relief it brings, nullifying my fool status. She will be lying in a hospital but at least I am not a fool. I am not a fool.

The room, as wide as the QE2, sways as I stand up quickly, the window latch opens; air and car noises rush in. Papers flurry in motion like frenzied snow. I trip over a can of Heineken, which rolls beneath the bed. The room slides; my feet rock, legs buckle. I feel suddenly old. Through fluttering curtains something blue, almost fragile, flicks through the air, landing delicately on a roll of film. A dragonfly in the lightest colour of blue hangs there. The blue looks as if it will fade into itself any second and emerge translucent white. This dragonfly clutches the top edge of the roll of film, hanging perpendicular to its sides. I move over to look closely, wobbling as I near it. It flies away and seems to vanish.

I think of the dragonfly as I leave, carrying the rolls of film. I can even imagine it clinging to my dark hair, its excreta sticking to my scalp.

Darkness. People like barriers cross in front of me, surrounding me with stale sweat. Men call from restaurants, wanting me to eat their steak and their *moussaka*, drink their *retsina* rather than across the street, somewhere else. I search for the photo developers that the hotel recommended. Darkness makes the men like shadows bending over each other in the restaurants and bars. The street carries the stench of meat freshly thrown from the market. I hand in the rolls of films. An hour. It is important to see her face again.

"The Plaka," Jude had said, "– shopping. Andy, please stay here as I won't be long. I want to get you something and you only get in the way."

A good excuse, it seems now. I loved the Plaka when we went yesterday; it made me dream of becoming a gnarled backgammon player hunched over in the gutter drinking espresso, watching the ephemeral world pass by, not caring about my street busking and earning a living. I can't imagine where she is.

We had walked down to Hephaestus's temple as the skeletal cats exited for the night, and bought a bright blue shawl from one of the shops opposite. I said it was the colour of her eyes; she'd laughed and said she hadn't realized I was such an old romantic. My eyes never leave her; maybe she's taken herself from me deliberately as a lesson, to experience freedom.

I stand in a square listening to music coming from upstairs. A light breeze comes up from the coast. Shadows of people reach around corners. People come out of a downstairs door. At first I think the girl with her arm round the chap is Jude, but of course she isn't. The girl wears the face of someone about to make love: intense, earnest and unreal, her mouth open slightly and turned down, her eyes screwed up and nostrils flared. The man moves her away quickly.

We started our travels in Athens fourteen days ago, flying in on a delayed bumpy night-flight, and were herded through darkened and hot streets while sensible people lay sleeping. In the coach, Jude slept, while I looked out the window at every sight as we left the Piraeus, almost afraid to miss anything. I wanted to be able to discover what was hidden behind every orange shutter, every untidy barricade of trash cans, every car parked precariously at weird angles on corners. Under the pearly streetlights Athens late night heat rose to greet the sky, making the roads look like dustbowls, dry, hazy, faded as if stunned by the sun, slightly pallid. Washed, weather-worn like an old hat. A thin dog, in the uncanny and unreal light, crossed on his way home. Jude, asleep, puckered her lips as she shivered in dreams.

Jude in the hotel shower, water streaming down, her back turned, her body dipping forwards, my arms around her; her slightly startled face; Jude in the boat round Nafplio, hands deep in the blue water, her face glowing, her upturned nose burnt a vibrant red, the intense sky, the spooky cries of cormorants.

These are what I think about now walking these streets without her. I party with a newfound Greek friend in the street as a party floats down from the flat above, bringing with it noise, smoke and laughter.

Someone is sick in a gutter near a trash pile. Well-dressed evening restaurant-goers pass disdainfully as I lift another Red Bull to my mouth and feel immediately nauseated as it courses down my throat. Everyone laughs hysterically as only people who don't know each other well can, talking in a variety of languages about football, British girls and the tightness of jeans, while heat gathers in the street, gathers around our feet, and rises insidiously to scratch at our eyeballs. A voice from the right says hello and a man passes me a joint. He has a face like a pixie, tiny and bright. English. More people enter the square, rush up the stairs of a nearby house after knocking twice. The party swells the flat. People are leaning out of the building, hanging over the window frames, pushing at the brick as if to take just one more person. Monotonous music pulsates along the pathways in my head, insinuating into my flesh like images of Jude. Deep thump of electronic drums, too perfect to be acceptable. I hate sounding so old.

Her image washes like thick liquid over my eyes, into my sockets and down the slopes of my cheeks, moving, changing, reshaping, saturating me. I open my eyes for a second and look up at the balcony of partygoers – a face staring at me, eyes like blue ice floes, whites shocking, hair blonde and dazed. If I blinked long enough could Jude reform before me, slide from the images over my eyes and stand in front of me?

Once she told me when she was making love that she felt she was like a butterfly flying above her head, that coming had been a transcendent experience and she had felt above and beyond herself. But this wasn't with me.

It was just two days ago that she had told me about Richard and his disappearance; her words coming soft and slow in a honeyed-little-girl voice as we lay in the hotel bed having just made love. Just the day before we had re-entered Athens after circumnavigating Greece: Mycenae, Toulon, Corinth Canal, lunch dabbling our toes in the Aegean at a restaurant before the ferry for Patras, thunderstorms over Olympia, wandering the ruins under the clear light of warm day, Delphi at night under red clouds, eating sticky *koulouria* in the town square and listening to dogs trot home howling. Heat from the window, a slight breeze, covers off, our minds open and our bodies vulnerable; her words crept inside me like shame. I filled up gradually like a balloon with her words.

She said that he had made her feel like this a few times, though what different thing he did that no one else had she didn't know, but it had made her unable to forget him. She said it was like a fluke, this feeling, an accident of nature. He wasn't any better in bed than anyone else. In every partner after him she had waited for that feeling to happen again, to arise out of herself, free, hovering, imagining herself with wings, soft and gentle like a butterfly, gently teasing the air with her flapping, rising with dust through the air, carrying herself on motes of light, before tumbling back to flesh, smiling.

Richard had then vanished some months after they had broken up. As Jude spoke, languidly, carefully, her arm reached back along the top of her head as if smoothing something down, as if she had rehearsed this many times in her head. He'd done this exact trip with his girlfriend of the time and at some point along the journey by coach around Greece had disappeared – Jude was never told exactly where. She said she tried to imagine his shape vanishing as he ran the track at Delphi, or a pillar at Hera's Temple at Olympia opening him up and swallowing him. Or maybe just the streets of Athens took him. She stood up at that point and walked naked to the window. Sweat trickled down her back. I sniffed the space she had left impregnated with her sweat and shape in the hollow of the bed. He could be out there, she said, hidden in the smog and the heat and the shadows rising from the hills. She worried about him. He'd been gone a year. The whole time we had been together. Then she smiled and I lurched inward, suddenly tasting bile. The taste of fear, the smell of loneliness; the immensity of space around me. I had never felt it before.

Suddenly my small Greek friend, Ed, walks away, "Where you going?" I shout, bile once more filling my throat. I've grown used to his face. He makes a motion with his right hand to indicate going for a piss. I smile and relax, covering the bile with fresh Red Bull from a new can. He returns from the darkened alley behind the square with a girl, whom he is glad to see, even though she doesn't stop talking in Greek. He looks at me and shrugs his shoulders.

"Andy, you come with Gina and me," he says, "A group of us are heading to Cape Sounion on the coast. Someone is performing. Much fun. Everyone in Athens will be there." He races away back to the alley and I hear a car. People scream and move rapidly out of the way as a car lurches into the square with my Greek friend behind the wheel. An American Cadillac convertible. He grins at my surprised face. "You like?"

"It's yours?"

"Of course, Andy. Get in, Gina."

"Everyone will be in their best cars tonight circling the city! Get in. Tonight we celebrate... Gina, what is it we celebrate?" Gina shrugs her shoulders. He laughs. "We celebrate! We will learn what soon enough! Who knows where we'll end?" They wait while I collect my photos and then we are gone.

At Mycenae, where the wind left scratch marks on our faces, Jude slipped away on one of the many pathways. I found her in Agamemnon's tomb way down the hill. She said she liked being alone in such a place, where somehow you felt overawed – by the tomb, by the height of the hill where Mycenae lay, tucked into the mountainside like a child lying with its mother, and remnants of the civilization, like leftover food from a party. The colours of the day were beige and grey. Beige the ground, beige the weeds cut and torn by the wind, darker beige the earth and grey the sky, littered with black clouds. She said it made her want to cry, to see it like this, so raw, exposed.

Tourists walked, heads bowed into the wind while buzzards screeched above. It wasn't like Delphi where the sky had been the lightest blue and Jude said she felt light like chiffon. Here I bent into the wind and looked for her, past the stones, up top, then back and down to the beehive of the Tomb where I found her leaning against a wall looking upwards, arms crossed and one foot treading firmly on the other, enraptured. While I was taking a picture of her, I could hear the room echoing and someone bumped into me, knocking my arms. That jolted shot will be in those rolls of film just like every other shot I took of her. It was a strange place, the Tomb; it made me think that we were all sharing this but what was it? I looked at these people in their shorts, white blouses and wondered if I'd ever bump into them in the world ever again. We sang like drinking pals on the coach.

I try to open the photos but Gina stops me, grabbing them. Jude's absence makes me think I invented her.

I feel the breeze immediately and a lightness. The roads are full of teenagers and twenty-somethings leaning out of Beetles, Golfs and Renaults. We are the only ones in a Cadillac, Gina in the front seat drinking from a can. We pass the police sitting on the edge of the road but no one stops us. The cars circle like red Indians following a trail of wagons. We circle two or three times, stopping sometimes to sing under trees or to talk. Everyone is smiling, shouting like it's a rodeo. It's bizarre. I loll in the back of the Cadillac, unbuckled, unbelted, without gravity, without a trajectory. A breeze could throw me, or a dragonfly could catapult me skywards.

I feel useless. At home I would try to entertain these people. I miss not being able to. Jude says I am alive when I am on show, when I entertain the crowds with my stilt-walking and fire-eating. I watch her watching me and watching the crowd. She says me swallowing fire is a turn-on for her. I come home and she makes me lick her with my kerosene mouth, before letting me make love to her. I wish I were on my stilts, fire-eating for these people. On my stilts I am powerful.

As we circle like performers round the roads of Athens, I try not to think of Jude and empty hotel beds and a woman who was barely there, who preferred chasing vanishing boyfriends to me. I like to drink. The Athens air is grimy. It tenses me. I twist the can of Red Bull round in my hand like I am strangling a chicken.

Fireworks and crackers shoot into the sky as we leave, and in the distance begins the slow build-up whine of police sirens, then Gina shouting. For ages we ride round and round. At one point we nearly run over a cat, which makes Ed laugh crazily.

"Just relax," says Ed. "It will be a great party. Big party. Have a drink or sleep." We went to Sounion, Jude and I, along with the rest of our reddening compatriots on the coach tour. Cape Sounion is less than an hour's drive from Athens, they said. A temple to Poseidon on a promontory. One more step and you'd be in the sea, wading with islands. It is quite wonderful.

Gina says we will be there for dawn and this excites me. I saw it at dusk with Jude, boats on the lilac horizon, little dotted islands. Jude had stood at the edge, looking over the Aegean, and felt, so she said, like Penelope waiting for Odysseus. The Greeks have always stood watch over the sea; watched its changing colours. We looked for Byron's signature and there it was. Hundreds of people look for it daily. Aren't we tourists like parasites, following each other round the sites like stitches in a hem? But these things have to be seen. How else can you see them but as a tourist? You cannot live in every place you visit.

I try to sleep. They play music while the breeze increases as darkness is penetrated, bringing with it vibrant smells of oranges, fresh leaves, sea-brine. We leave Athens noisily. I don't sleep much, for I am busy remembering Jude and how we ate squid at a wayside restaurant before climbing the ferry to the Peloponnese, dabbling our toes in the clear water and thinking the Aegean was a dream. An unreal sky overhead. We inhabit the space of a picture inside the head of a dreamer. The space expands as we move about inside it —as our epidermis – the toes, fingers – reacts to the coldness— clambering over it like mad children. Cold washed over us and the picture now grows and swells and it looks more unreal looking back on it than it did at the time; that we were truly there, that these things happened. I will look back on this car ride into an empty Greek countryside and it will feel more exciting as a memory than it does now, as I sit here smelling of smoke and alcohol. Gina snores.

"Nearly there!" says Ed turning round, making the car swerve. The hills fade and the distance glows, the hills wear a halo. The sea appears again. We are at Sounion. Gina wakes.

I walk about the empty site; I could never believe it could be like this. No tourists, no coaches pumping out diesel. No girlish Jude laughing, racing up to the stone pillars, her skirt tucked into her knickers, shouting out information about the temple – the mention of it in Homer, me following, relishing the glimpses of her bare flesh. Sometimes you have the taste of someone in your mouth and I can taste her now. I can feel the crevices of her body, taste the sweatiness between her legs, on my tongue when she lets me get truly intimate with her body. I miss her touch on my skin, her presence like a touch on my eyes. I can see her but I ache for something more substantative than my memory. Flesh is better than a memory, even though the memories have the power. I taste fear again. Fear of never seeing her. Suddenly my body is drained of drunkenness and I wonder what I am doing here and what I should do about Jude.

The temple is covered in blue light glowing in places like a radioactive star. The day is beginning. Gina and Ed are laughing. "See! Everyone but everyone is here!" I reach back to the car and grab my photos. Gina looks at me as if I shouldn't concern myself with them now. I take a quick look and see the theatre at Epidaurus but no image of Jude, before Gina takes my arm and pulls me towards the Temple.

Far below the temple people are swimming in the water. It's a long walk down to them. Almost the same set of people who circled Athens are here in small groups, running over the rocks, the same laughter, the same inane drunken conversations. I wander through, listening to snippets of Greek, English and French. The people are young, though there's a grey haired chap standing on a rock high over everyone else. People are running over to the nearby Athena's temple, bottles roll to the floor, lighted cigarettes wave in a dance-like procession, like a procession of lighted saints in a Spanish town.

Gina hands me another drink. Drunkenness washes through my body once more. She's small and cheeky, with cow's eyes. Ed watches. I would have preferred to stay back in Athens wandering the Plaka, like those stringy cats; waiting for the sun to rise, to drink espresso in the gutter like an old man. Our flight is tomorrow. I should get back, to wait by the phone in case Jude rings. What if she returns to the hotel room to find I'm gone? I can't bear this not knowing. Her absence is like a slap in my face. Our flat without her is unimaginable.

I wander down, carefully, steadily, following Ed. Down by the rocks a couple are kissing. The girl is nearly falling into the water. I imagine her naked, leg stretched out, his hands reaching for her wet crotch. But she's not. I am trapped in this freedom that Jude's absence and night have given me. It is just like a rope around my body, binding me more closely than bars; it is almost as if the sky is my boundary.

In this half-light many shapes remind me of Jude. Everyone looks like Jude. She is here in millions, like shattered pieces of glass. My eyes are disfigured by freedom; all I see is her face – the scar on her eyebrows, her rich skin radiating warmth. I want to throw stones at these false idols.

Water on my shoes. I look up and there is Jude, smiling wryly. How can that be? Everyone will be here – Ed had said. Light creeps through the fissures in the sky as she moves towards me, wearing a yellow t-shirt with a fat strawberry printed upon it I have never seen before and her hair is tied up unusually in a ponytail. She is shattered glass made whole. My hungry eyes feast upon her. She is real. I didn't make her up. The night retreats quickly.

She touches my arm, says "How did you find me here? I should've guessed I could never escape you."
    "I didn't know you wanted to."
    She smiles. "It was an accident. I didn't mean it. I'm sorry."
    "Where you been?"
    "Looking. Out. I needed a break."
    "I've been going crazy."
    "I know. Sorry." She takes my hand. We walk. "I found him."
    "Who?"
    "Richard."
    "I don't believe it! That's impossible."

When she moves her arm from mine, looks back, and smiles at a distant part of the darkness, something moves out in the sea; a light faintly glowing. Waves licking rocks like tongues on lollipops. My throat constricts. Fear again. Perfection is impossible. We all compromise. I bend like potter's clay for her. She moulds me with her very breath. She touches me and I shape into elasticity. Nothing is ever how you want it. No one is ever how you want them. I wanted Jude without ghosts but they are with her in her every footstep. She has been following Richard but really he has inhabited her pores like bacteria.

"I saw him today in a shop."

"In Athens?"

"He was working there. Just working. Nothing had happened to him. He'd just decided to stay, to be here and not somewhere else."

She smiled a smile of sexual intensity; so incongruous, so intense, so content. I remember the pale dragonfly. The butterfly of her imagination. They could be hovering round her now like she was a Chinese lantern. On her outstretched fingers pale delicate blue wings flap in the night breeze, glowing against her fingers.

"You slept with him?"

She says nothing, turns to walk away from me, into the growing light. I trip over stones as I look up, walking towards her but she has gone. Gina and Ed are laughing. Above, cars pull up, motorcycles and mopeds. An army of partygoers emerge. A boat starts quickly to the side of me, a guttural heaving; everyone runs down the hill, racing, jumping over rocks and swinging round dying olive trees. All around are people shouting.

Dawn, like a precocious, spoiled child, is growing sharp and fat. Light settles on the hills, on the trees, on the land like a vibrant effervescent covering of dust, picking out contours and undulations. The sky changes from glowing blue to translucent pink yellow grey sliced through with shades of blue. Everything looks still. The sky lightens in seconds, the land lightens. My eyes squint, yet the sun isn't in view. Light illuminates my arms, and I feel as if I were in a disco picked out by radiant light. There is Jude, smiling still. I race after her. I touch her. She is with a man. I recognize him. He's well-dressed, light beard on his chin, hair scorched by the sun. She whispers in his ear and he turns to me. I feel still caught in the spotlight, jagged, frozen and moving statically like a shadow puppet. Her flesh in my hand. I touch my mouth with her sweat, and lick my palm. Her eyes crinkle like she's eaten something nasty.

She says, "Go home." Gina reaches me. We are all slow motion. I feel like screaming. Gina smiles to Jude. They say they are heading out to the islands.

"But you can't go," says Jude, "You've a flight in…" she looks at her watch, "three hours. Poor babe." She laughs and walks slowly away looking back over her shoulder as she descends to the boat.

I follow her. I have to follow her – I cannot be alone. It frightens me more than I ever believed possible. I trip on the rocks. My feet stand in water. The light returns to normal as she and the boat head out into the rising sun. She leans on Richard. She has gone. A dot in the distance, as small as a dragonfly.

The light is ordinary now, boring even. New-born daylight steals my strength. I should hitch a lift on a returning moped to Athens, to the hotel room, to the airport, to England. But instead my knees loosen; I flop into the water as if boneless, dropping photos like confetti from my pockets. I lie here face down in the water, tasting salt in my throat. Photos – a Grecian sky; of a sweet face among many less appealing; of the view of the harbour from our window at Nafplio; of a sidewards-posing body in a hazy focus – arc away from me, drifting with the current, while water pushes over my legs, my arms, my back; as the sun rises blazing, scorching, making the sky as white as the sclera of an eye, blocking out the lightest blue.

Moth-Dust

She became aware of moths as a child at a campsite deep in the Black Forest surrounded by enormous closely guarding pine trees. In the toilets, the showers, hundreds of moths clustered on the lights. Every moth in the vicinity must have been there – beige, orange, grey, always floury, shaking dust from their wings in an energetic frenzied motion. Such mindless propulsion towards heat, light – she was frightened of their movements, of the energy they generated with their wings. They flew in jagged motion at her face. She screamed. More flew at her face. They were out of control, attacking her; her mother pulled her away from the centre of the room.

In her dreams the moths follow her to the showers. Night showers in a rain of moths. She remembers that first night dreaming of moths, waking up screaming as one crawls down her throat: a solitary moth creeping downward towards darkness, the dry gossamer taste in her mouth, gagging. They are monsters, their thin filigree wings teasing her nostrils, flapping with a contradictory precise chaotic motion. They fly under her chin, settle on her eyes. As she wipes away one moth, another lands on her arms, legs, breast. There are moths on her knees, feet, moths landing on her cheeks, fluttering at her neck with tiny vampire teeth.

She hated trees after that. Dark trees full of fairytale eyes. The trees harbour the moths; the trees harbour something she cannot control. The trees can move and come at her – the stories she reads tell her so. The dark holds the moths. They shoot out of the dark silence like bullets. She blinks; she closes her eyes to them, in case they bite into her eyeballs, chew them between their soft wings, desiccate the pulp of the eye, lacerate like a whip mark. Ulcerating. Touch of wing against eyeball. Sharp, like the side of a piece of paper, cutting softly, stridently down her iris. Slicing her pupil in two, like a knife into hardened eggs.

Moths come to the window and through the window when she isn't aware the window is open. They jitter to her with limpid wings. More moths. Moths warming to her; desperate for her. It is as if they can sense her skin, smell her blood. They need her. They are cold without her. Moths going crazy around a lamp. The noise of wings on hot metal. And burning.

She takes precautions: she covers her bed in netting, rarely opens her window on summer evenings and sometimes doesn't turn on the lights. She knows the house in darkness. When she hears the tremors of wings, she freezes. But the moths are canny; they close down their wings and sneak in through cracks and gaps, drawn to even a tiny light switched on for the briefest of seconds; they are unerring, mechanical, fluttering. They seek her and cover her. All night they lay upon her. Moths on top of moths. Wings outstretched.

She dreams of moths when she feels most powerless: when love defeats her, when people fail her, or she fails herself, or when she is most unable to help herself and she feels adrift on emotions that she cannot control; when she stands restless in the middle of a room, waiting for the door, the phone, the inbox tinkle; when she is waiting for something to happen, fearing that nothing will ever happen ever again. They come into her mind then, when she needs to grab at something solid but they feel like sand grains escaping between her fingers. They come to taunt her; they come to bring her down. During daylight she thinks the moths have invaded her insides and are vibrating frantically inside her belly and down her intestinal tract. She swears she feels them while she sleeps. She can smell their presence in her nightmare sweats; where they've flapped, where they've defecated, where they slivered. In her dreams she is eaten whole by moths and all that is left of her is moth-dust.

The Hand of Fatima

Irlam likes to pat the necks of camels. He says they are beautiful creatures.

I say camels are ugly, and smell.

Irlam loves the desert.

I say the desert is just a patch of ground there to make you burn and starve.

Irlam's been here before. He says he knows better than me. He wants to be a hero, he wants to be an upstanding man, a guide to the helpless, the unknowing. Irlam tries to fool me with his romantic wonder and Lawrence of Arabia nonsense. I only refer to Irlam by his surname. He thinks it sounds more exotic than John.

I think Irlam is full of shit. Especially now as we stand here alone and suddenly very lost and the morning has hardly begun. And I can't find anything to make a drink in.

When I woke this morning the first thing I noticed was Ahmed's empty hillock. Ahmed, our guide, our man of practicalities and knowledge.

Last night, as we slept, Ahmed must have left us. We had been camping out. Irlam said we should feel the desert sky on our faces, the intense cold, the purity, the sound of the sky. Me in one sleeping bag, covered up from the cold, Irlam next to me. Ahmed was Bedouin, Irlam said, he could watch from beyond. I said he'd freeze. Irlam said he could cope with that, he's Bedu! Ahmed just shrugged his shoulders and went away from us, away from the fire, to a hillock of sand.

Irlam brushed down his shirt and said he's gone to cleanse himself, or something. I point out that his possessions have gone, the spare flask, his chained spicy amulet and his sleeping bag.

We wait. The city is somewhere west. Irlam had been hoping to get to the centre of the desert with Ahmed's help. The sand stretches for miles and miles. This is the desert. I stand, awed by the glass-like chill of the air, the infinitesimal grains of sand and the geometry of the horizon, wondering if there is a heart to it.

Tall Irlam. Thin, gangling. He stands at the edge of the desert and surveys, one arm tucked at right-angles behind his back, the other hand protecting his eyes from the sun.

We'd been going deeper into the desert. As if searching for something but it feels like going round and round in widening circles. Would we ever come out again? Irlam says he knows what we are doing. I have to believe him. But now, without Ahmed?

Been through the desert on a horse with no name – that is what he was singing as he came towards me, when we first met, looking slightly drunk. People scattering, looking bemused. He latched onto me. I was white, young, vulnerable.

Irlam says I'll do.
Irlam says I am pretty enough for his purposes.

I smile. He kicks the sand, turns round and round, looks up into the sky and mumbles something in Arabic, a phrase he'd picked up from the back of a chocolate bar and had got Ahmed to pronounce it for him. Yet being who he is, what he is, he has no idea what it means. He just repeats it over and over like he is saying something profound. He has charm, knowledge, wit. He has purpose. I do like him though. Poor Irlam, poor boyish Irlam.

I pack up our belongings. Irlam stares at the horizon. I miss Ahmed's conspiratorial smiles.

We have jeeps; we can drive till we find the city or find what it is people look for in the desert. Irlam says that is just bullshit. Nothing can be found in the desert but sores and scorpion bites and dark nights of the soul. I smile enigmatically saying nothing, knowing that's precisely the point. But it's all clichés! He says he hates my Mona-lisa smile. Mona-Lisa was a boy, he says, making a dervish shape, whirling. Arms outstretched.

Irlam is a romantic fool.

We have water. We can survive. Aren't you glad, I say, that I said I loathed camels? I look at the jeep. Battered, hardly salubrious but compared to camels...

Camels are eco-friendly, Irlam replies, standing on a hillock pointing east, Sousse must be that way.

We'd been there before. It was where we met, outside the Medina walls. Me standing there, him singing. Sousse. On the beach there where that inept tourist train stops, there where Andre Gide lost his virginity, he tells me. Andre who?

Sometimes he likes to wander away from me and watch me without him. I know I am being watched so I smile enigmatically. I know what he is capable of. I go with him. I play up to him and feed his fantasies. Out here, far from help, phones, Starbucks, the Sunday papers, you have to trust someone.

At the caves of Matmata he was in his element pretending to be Luke Skywalker, pretending to be Darth Vader as a boy. He grinned at the people who live there. And handed out CDs like a missionary. Play these, play these. They walked away smiling strangely, shaking their heads at his lack of understanding.

Without him here I don't know what I would do. I'd be lost.

Lost in Sousse! He laughs at my ineptitude. Lost in Sousse.

Once, he confesses, I was lost in Sousse. A guide, just after I had arrived, we are all green at that point, took me deep into the heart of the Medina, saying he would show me the grand Mosque. I had a map but it was useless, the streets are a maze of twists and turns. I was frightened but pretended I wasn't. After all who am I to agree with cultural stereotypes and believe this man would lead me astray?

Cultural stereotypes, I say, like what?

That Arabs are untrustworthy, that Americans know what they are doing, that the English are snobbish.

They're not true?

He says nothing but looks at me: Irlam unamused.

What did you do? I say finally.

I smiled a lot and watched every corner, but I'd rather not talk about it. He turns away and jumps into the jeep. Are you coming? He can't get the jeep started – the gearbox for a moment confuses him as if he has forgotten how to work it.

Been through the desert on jeep with no name.

I wonder what it's like to be really alone out here.

He told me he would show me the real North Africa. He said he was an expert. It sounded plausible. Irlam was a student of architecture, he said. Studying was his passion. He revelled in the beauty of knowledge. He'd point things out to me, fill me in on what I had missed. He says it's not safe for me to travel alone. With a man you are protected. Without me what would Irlam do? He is so like a boy with his pouting full lips and his frazzled dark hair and his smile that makes me want to please him. He tells me about places I have never been. He can show me experiences that tourists never see. He says that if I stay with him I will be rewarded. I promise, he said, looking directly at me, to look after you.

I don't need looking after.

It's dangerous alone, he says. Having you with me is important. The most important thing.

We have seen oases at dawn, rotting palm trees, waterfalls and pools of Tamarza, sand dunes like mountains at Douz. Markets where the sandals were made by a small beardless man whose eyes never looked at me, who handled my feet as if precious cargo – he reeked of urine and leather; we have seen villages of Sidi Bou Said – the blue, the white buildings, the hypnotic skies – and empty fishing villages as prayers were said in hillside mosques, overlooking caramel rocks. We have stood on cliff edges above villages, above the sea, just breathing in the crisp air of the continent.

We have seen horses emaciated and falling, Berber children posing for pictures, the sun rising on the desert which quite stunned us. We have seen many things, Irlam and I. And he is still a mystery to me. I have seen him beat a boy who came to him for change. I have seen him dance at sudden parties like a wild man. I have seen him screaming in French to men who came towards us in a village, who wouldn't leave us alone. I have seen his face red to bursting as he shouted and screamed and gesticulated until the men walked away back to the bar. He enjoys these things. I have seen him so angry at the phone system in one hotel that he hit his fist against the wall, leaving a hand-sized hole.

We get lost searching for the city, we travel in circles. I trust he will get us there. I need a bath and a good bed. We criss-cross the sand, passing our tread marks. We make our circles wider and wider, increasing our radius. He will get us there. I trust being with him.

Sometimes Irlam goes as far out into the night away from me as he can and just sits there. I have no idea what he thinks as he sits there looking out across the black horizon. He likes to be charming but sometimes he looks morose. I still like him. I wonder if my like is more survival dependency than real affection.

We meet up with some westerners: faces so tanned. They are a party from the tourist areas, people Irlam despises but today he welcomes them. I hear him getting advice about directions. He talks in German. He says he is an expert on the nomadic tribes of North Africa, he says he comes from San Francisco. He advises them to avoid Djerba. They tell me about their hotel, about the service on little trays at poolsides, about meals delicately prepared: lemon-cooked fish and couscous and salads, how they play tennis in the mornings after wandering the harbour's attractions, after drinking espresso surrounded by orange sellers and hawkers desperate to get you inside their shop. Everyone wants something, they say, everyone wants something from you. They would sell their soul to make money out of you. I yearn for the tourist train to safety.

Irlam looks out for me, Irlam needs me too. I cannot leave him. I say good-bye to the tourists in the immaculate jeeps. And we travel on, to Sousse. Irlam whistles and bangs the steering wheel, cursing as the jeep hits against rocks.

Sousse is ugly in many ways. It is good to be back. I climb the Ribat to see the whole of the town. I can look down upon the forbidden Mosque. Irlam said Sousse was a place of geometry – squares upon squares, reflected patterns in buildings, heavy rectangular doorways opening into hermetic cells for warrior-monks. From here Sousse looks like a chaotic mass of beige/white and eggshell blue doorways disappearing into the horizon. Down there is the twisty non-geometric Medina. Chaos enclosed by geometry. Then a mass of industrialization, fat oil tankers slicing through the sea.

The grand Mosque, he says, and the Kasbah, and then this house, deep in the Medina, where someone I know lives. We will visit. You must taste his qahwa. He will be most upset if I do not visit him.

Socks, bed linen, nightwear hanging outside a shop, a front full of shoes, a shop selling leather jackets – we go inside the Medina along the straight street that runs parallel. People staring at us as we travel. Scrawled pictures of symbolic fish pinned everywhere, and the protecting Hand of Fatima. Then he makes us turn right, inwards, into the centre. Irlam in front, me trailing. He says, Don't catch their eye, don't trust them if you speak to them. We go along straight for a while, turn inwards again, then straight, then up. There are little alleyways everywhere.

Shouts of English? English! We push forward like combatants into the crowd. Irlam strides forward. We go deeper, he shouts. We turn corners, passing Hands of Fatima painted, mosaiced, carved on ornate doorways. We go deeper. Crowds thin out. We are the only white faces. The streets narrow. We pass open doorways revealing women shunting carpet weavers, the smell of dyed sheepskins, raw sheepskins. The chatter of women. The lethargy of hovering men. More corners, going left past orange tasselled banners. Deeper.

I mark the banner. I mark patterns and colours, fan-shaped palms, aromatic smells drifting from open windows, thinking left then right, right again. Keep track. Up a hill. I can see no sky. The houses reach over us. Irlam is moving so fast. As purposeful as a scorpion, for once. Or is it more bravado? Does he know where he is going? It is all so confusing.

Wait, wait, I cry. Slow down.

The street gets even narrower, fewer people. We turn into a small square with a large drain in the centre, all the streets just here seem to end and flux into the drain. Beige squares. So many streets end here. To one side is a large woman. As imposing as a Sumo wrestler. We are arrested for a moment by her screaming. She lifts up her layers of skirts, Not Bedu, says Irlam, shaking his head. She squats, layers of linen, tied, wrapped, hanging from her waist, gathered up into her arms. Her face is open, dark dark and filthy – but her head is similarly wrapped. She stinks. She squats silently for some time before a long river of piss runs into the drain. It is as if she is pissing into the navel of the Medina and her urine spirals to the centre. She begins to scream and shriek once more. And moves towards us. She sees me, takes a stride closer, skirts creasing. Irlam puts his arm around my shoulders and hurries me forward.

Streets straight then curved. Walls painted green. Fish symbols. Doors with black engraved patterns like the ornate hennaed hands of the market sellers. We bend right, move straight, bend left, snaking through streets, feeling as if we're getting tighter and tighter to the heart of the Medina, squeezed into its centre. Irlam stops, turns round, says this way. I ask if he's sure. He says of course he is. We back track, take the right instead of the left turning.

Come on, Delise. I try to walk quicker, looking backwards, forwards, always ready to run, looking for friendly faces, white faces, tourist faces. I want Irlam to stop, I want us to turn back, not zigzag endlessly into the centre of the Medina. I don't know if Irlam is lost as I am. I want to go back.

I wish Ahmed were here to show me what these painted symbols mean. I wish I could see the sky and feel the chill of the desert night. Delise is tired, I say, tired. There is a beach here. Gide, I shout. Let's stand on the beach where Gide...

Later. Nearly there. It will be worth it.

He points to something round a corner. There he is, Irlam, white shirt, black jeans, red rucksack with the words Ascent emblazoned in black lettering. Irlam smiling. Irlam happy. Paint is peeling from the walls, narrow doorways, no sky, an exit left, an exit right. A shape fills a doorway to the right. Beside him a black hand of Fatima. The shape filling the alley way to the left coughs. Irlam is chattering, telling me stuff I cannot hear. I move towards him, he backs away. I step closer, he steps back. He's still talking and smiling, calling me forward with a precise motion of his hand. There are three exits – Irlam stands in one. Behind him I can see an alleyway opening out to the sky. A man comes from behind him, startling him. At first he looks frightened then he smiles, taps the man in a knowing way on the shoulder and walks past him. Then I hear the sound of Irlam running up the alleyway. Where he once stood another man stands. I watch Irlam's shape vanish as the corner takes him away. Irlam escaping. Irlam leaving me here. I can't even shout out, I can't think what he is doing.

The other exits are blocked by shapes that show themselves now as men. They come towards me, head downwards towards me, like bulls charging. I can feel them closing, just a slight breeze of light between their shapes. They encircle me, touch my hair, I can just see their teeth as I lift up to look at them. But I am too scared to really see them, to really see what Irlam has led me to, what Irlam has abandoned me to.

The alleyways close in, buildings cover me, the Hand of Fatima to the side swells. I close my eyes, and then open my eyes in fear of not knowing everything, of being blind to the inevitable. All I see is the Hand of Fatima, and taste their smell in the back of my throat, their sweat and their labours, gagging on the astringency of aftershave. I can feel their touch on my face, their sweat on my skin. I can't scream. I want to close my eyes, I want to get out of here. I daren't look at their faces, I cannot say what sort of men they are for I close my eyes again and put up my hands to keep them away, to knock their fingers and smell away from me. I push against them. Push hard against them. Keep pushing till the smell is that of the street once more.

I find Irlam some months later, working as a guide for the tourist trade. He is alone, standing by the Matmata caves, as the tourists intermingle with the cave dwellers. He is twisting a wooden cross pendant in his hand.

Delise, I say, Delise. He seems surprised to see me, looks up at me, shielding his eyes against the sun. We say nothing for a while. I am expecting him to ask what happened. I am expecting a logical explanation for him running away. Eventually I ask why he had left me there. He says he didn't know.

Bullshit.

He says nothing, looks away. Then, he says, I don't know why I did it.

Money? It was deliberate.

It wasn't arranged like that. They were people I knew.

You said you would make sure no harm came to me. You said I was important to you. What did you expect to get from it? I can't believe you did it.

I don't know what to say. I have no excuses. I am sorry. He is afraid to look at me. He is afraid of his own behaviour. To hurt him in return would be like hurting a child because it spat on your clothes. I don't know what to say to him anymore. I don't know how to explain that what he did was unforgivable.

I walk away.

Did they hurt you? He shouts standing up. Are you ok? I worried.

The memory-smell of their cheap western aftershave: stinging, vivacious; the rough snagging touch of calloused skin; musty stench of old clothes, arms wrapped round me like binds, and the memory of the bile-fear in my belly. These are my dreams.

I always see me running through alleyways. My dreams are seared as if burnt with the image of the Hand of Fatima and blue doors and streets and the palm tree on the right, shaped like a fan, followed by a turn to the left, into the main square, back to the Mosque, back to the main part of the city, to trains cutting through streets and people shouting English? English? And the symbolic fish are always mouthing.

I dream of blue skies and squatting pissing women and Irlam smiling. The men were surprised that I could run from them. My dreams are like detectives: they tell me what I could never know: revealing the men's faces, as is Irlam's intent and Irlam's cowardly running away.

The dreams show Irlam as he was when I first met him, singing, *Been through the desert on a horse with no name. Got to get out of the rain.* And drunk.

A Song of Need

There are three women, three sisters, three friends, three women who happen to know of each other, are maybe connected or maybe not. Three lives.

Lem has a man who keeps her at the peak of sexual need; he touches her gently, but never fucks her how she wants to be fucked.

It may as well be a tower, where Lem lives. She's there and when he's there he watches her every hand movement, her every sneeze, every eyelash flicker. She can't make a movement without him seeing her. And when he leaves, she remains momentarily free. He leaves to do man's stuff, he says, *earn the money to keep her in good clothes*. But she never goes out. She floats about the house in finery of red silks and purple muslin, and dark velvets that melt on the touch. She hums songs and gazes from the high bay windows. Sometimes she plays old tunes on her guitar.

She is a woman in waiting.

When he fucks her, he plays with her, teasing, suggesting. He touches her cunt, she can barely hold her breath for thinking *maybe this time, this time he'll enter me*. Lem thinks: *Play with my cunt, play with me, lick me*. Instead, barely his breath warms the skin of her. His fingers thrust into her arsehole. She yelps and then without any kind of foreplay or gentleness, he thrusts his cock where his finger had been.

Sometimes he invites other men to where he goes.

She says nothing. She's not a leaving sort of woman. She hopes the other men will give her what he won't. but they don't; they follow his lead after first being surprised at the offer but he encourages them that it is genuine and they accept. His graciousness, his lack of jealousy. He sits and watches and watches her pained expression as they aren't gentle with her either.

And she never knows what force controls how she will be treated by him, what motion of chance. Her days are on the edge. The edge of need. To be constantly wanting. It is her every fibre this wanting, this need. It's like her flesh is electrified, shot through with bolts, hot blue bolts, from fingertips to sky. Lem can never forget that she needs. And her head hums with the song of need.

Tamar lies still in bed with sheets tightly wrapped round her. Every night she wraps the sheets, the shrouds of sleep. She lies still – she never moves, her breathing is regular and even. Every movement is careful and thought through. She even monitors the beat of her heart.

She monitors the depth of the sunrise: the timing, the vanishing. She lives over the motion of tides, and values her unencumbered horizon.

Her arms are sleek like pistons, the gleam of pistons oiled and polished. She has muscles to rival a man, and the mindset to rival a shark.

When day breaks she is running and running, she runs through a forcefield of her own creation. Nothing can touch her.

She passes someone drowning and waves, she passes gleeful smiles on passers by, she passes a carnival in motion and is too busy with her own expression of motion – arms pistoling up and down, head forward, forward motion – to stop, to climb on board to loosen her arms round the body of a human.

When Tamar was young, she tells people, she was experimental and wild and out there. She did wild things, she says, *Wild wild things.*

Her voice is clipped, her toe nails tidy and her skin sleek.

Her friends, Femi, and Bill, and Simon from the hills, don't believe her – *a wild side?* They laugh. *They were joyful times,* she says, *though I was scared, always scared. And rightly so. Tell us,* they say, *tell us these stories.* The bar behind tinkles. And laughter never reaches her ears.

But she can't even find the words to express the joy she once had. It is as if the words, the emotion, the force died inside her, stillborn even.

Her sleep at night is tight, motionless and guarded.

The other, Aliesha, lies still on a flat solid rock, guarded by angelic joyful faces. Shrouded and grey. Anonymous now in the enclosed gloom. No motion. Just the hum of rock.

The hum of rock.

Aftermath

Crows get shot at, crows steal lambs, crows foretell the future. She has a thing about crows.

Raucous winter crow-cries signal the end of summer. She counts the crows not the magpies. Doesn't think of luck. She likes to watch the crows. Their wings form right-angles as they hop and jump. Why don't they fly from place to place, why hop? Their hops are ungainly. They look ankle-bound – if they had heels their Achilles would have been slashed by blades.

A skull lies wind-cleansed, whiter than eyes. The crows ignore it. For now. A sheep-skull. No body. On the other side of the moor is a decomposing body of a sheep. No clean bones, only fresh kill fresh death flesh. Sickening. The crows hover. The crows cry. They've found this, as if they've searched the fields and the moor for it. Now they're plucking flesh, flesh torn from bone as if elastic.

Over granite rocks moss grows. With every damp spit of wind the moss grows. The birds sit and dig at it. Peck at it. She scatters the crows to sit. She brushes the stone, she sits. The day is greyed at the edges, sun lights the above sky, the firmament sky, the sky of heaven. The rock is shaped like a table. It has serrated edges where people who she can't even imagine once used it as a tool, a workbench, a holder of rocks. This is where she normally meets him. This is where she hums and jiggles her feet waiting for him, this is where she plans how she will keep him, thinking up schemes and tricks. She thinks she has all the tricks there can be: he will come up from behind her, quietly treading down gorse, releasing the scent of dull apricots into the grey sky. He will smile, he will call out, "Hey Sussie, gotcha!" She too will smile and take his arm, grabbing, grabbing it on the elbow and pull him to her and snuggle into his chest. This act of helplessness always makes him feel good and wanted. He grips her tighter and smiles, sliding himself next to her, breathing her in.

But she doesn't love him.

The crows hop sidewards noisily alongside of them, teasing, jostling, never serious.

There are always crows.

They're everywhere. As autumn dazzles and winter is hinted beneath the buried layer of hues of brown leaves, crows are hopping in lines like a search party of coppers. It's gone time. He's not coming. She cares that he stands her up but only for her pride.

Once she hid from him, on the far side, hidden by boulders but watching like a prying child. The crows fought buzzards over her head, the cows drifted, the sheep drooped in gorse bushes, a passing posse of skylarks chattered. It was summer and even from the moor heat rose like mist, like autumn mist that smothers the valley right now. He came; he walked high onto the moors. He stopped, he stopped smiling. He rubbed dirt from the front of his specially bought walking boots, brown leather, black ties. He had no dog for excuses. But then he didn't need them. He said he was free but she never believed any of them. Not any more. She would never follow him home to discover his lies, she would never listen at doors to hear to whom he spoke, what smiles and platitudes and soothing noises he gave to a hidden someone indoors, she never watched his private self carving lies from her stupidity; they weren't worth that but she used any other means of identifying these men who

166

smiled and lied their way into her life. Not all of them could fool her. Not now. Her life was one of precautions. And precautions and more precautions. She redressed herself daily, a seven veil dance in reverse, a recreation of self.

She had watched him sit there, she watched him pick his nose, fumble his balls through his trousers, she watched him scratch on the table granite seat and whistle and stare at the skylarks and the crows, look at his watch, stare at the horizon, at the direction from where he expected her to rise up the moor like Venus. She laughed how he wanted her so badly he would watch the sun vanish before the chill night rushed him home. She was long gone by then. She wished there was a way of watching him returning home. "Sussie," he would say the next day, "Where were you? I waited," and she would pander to him and pretend she was such a fool she'd got it mixed up and she could hear his voice relax and him sigh and believe her pathetic woman's scatty brain. She'd smile and arrange their next rendezvous.

His name was Mike and sometimes he suited her and sometimes not. Once she told him that she had missed him, once she'd called him darling and nearly vomited into the triangular-patterned pillow. Once she stroked him and smoothed him with touches as if love. He mistook her empty touches for real passion. And always, everywhere, untouched, unthought, was the unrealized shadow of someone she could no longer believe in.

Once she did tell him that she loved him, lying in that day's borrowed, paid for bed, the much lied upon sheets, changed but always the same. At first it had been hard to lie to him, after all he had been nothing but good to her. But she'd convinced herself she could do it, that it was important. With every lie, with every word of love, with every act of love she smiled for him, smiled to herself about what she was achieving, that she was marking for herself a presence in the universe. Every lie was like a recharge.

There was a time when she wasn't like this, when she believed and dreamed and acted with honour. She believed in honour. Now, in the aftermath of everything, honour was a lie and honour was for fools who didn't know what to do. Honour was a word she spat upon. The codes, rules, way of behaving, morals were nothing anymore, that meant fuck all, they meant straitjackets and dreams and stupidity. All the values she once believed in, everything she expected when people, men talked to her had changed. Nothing was what it seemed and so she could no longer be straight, geometric, knowable. She had to be hidden. And nihilistic in her pleasure. Tricksy and teasing and never serious, never real.

The crows peck at the body of the sheep, squawking, obvious, shiny black crows. Wings like iridescent blackened pearls; cries, voices as scorched as their wings. The night comes and she thinks she shouldn't like to be out here in this increasing numbing coldness. It's not somewhere to get caught alone.

The holes appear overnight. Between evening, as she left, descending to the valley to her home and existence, and early morning, when the sky seemed transparent and yet sliced with orange colours, shepherds warning, the ground subsides, caves away, disintegrates. Some of the holes are small, almost like footprints, some tentative, some thudding, insistent in strength. Other holes are like craters, like asteroid collisions, like bomb pits to slide sleighs down. The sheep avoid it. Some crows hop in and out of the footprints, looking for worms, for hidden things to pull and tug out, to tease out into the air. Other crows fly over and awkwardly fall into the holes, falling about themselves, wings upended and reflecting in the sharp sun.

At first she sits and looks at the holes, they encircle her. It is as if someone tall high in the sky had thrown missives down, like planes. She reasons what it could be – hailstones, man made? She reasons and gets nowhere.

The holes are rounded in shape, or oval or distended, the ground is friable where the shape had been moulded. She walks round them, jumping in them, looking up at the sky. Holes. The ground looks squashed, as if pressed down by giant hands, or swirling wind.

She sits on her table seat and surveys the view. The crows dance through, over, in and out of the holes, the sheep drift slowly, the crows seem to be laughing.

The holes are too many to count; she keeps getting lost in the order of where she had been and where she had yet to count. She runs in them, out of them, screaming with the pure mindlessness of movement, the thrill of rushing chemicals pulsing through her blood. Breathless now, hands on hips, more holes disappearing down the valley, she pauses before flinging herself down the inside of the next hole. Crows screaming in the air.

Clouds move over, wheatears squealing, protesting in the sky, the colours change, leaves bronzed, papyrus thin, disintegrating, pine trees dripping bleached needles, the ground beneath the trees is smothered by them. She moves from her table seat and scuffs in the pine needles, they cover her boots, they burrow like worms inside her boots. She moves down, looking into the trees, thinking about her house, the way she lives, thinking about Mike and those she doesn't name.

The crows are dancing, she's walking down from the ridge, descending to the trees, to the beech square that surrounds a moss-hidden cottage. The trees are half-naked, leaves sun-withered, tepid, hesitant colours, while those on the ground are orange, baroque, in drifts, in piles, scattered and heaped. She's watching the leaves, watching the pyramid shapes, wind catching them, lifting upwards and to the side, spoiling the shape, the symmetry, the perfection; the ridge descends, the crows are behind her and above her and crying suddenly and the ground is vanishing, caving, imploding. Her arms flay out, she catches grass, mud, leaves between her nails, her arms slashed by brambles, gorse, feet capsized, body capsized.

Her cry is covered by the desperate banter of the crows, the sound, the movement of their blue-slashed wings beating the sky, the wind and the clouds smothering, laughter of crows. And the chill of nothingness.

With Phantoms Still

Coming back and I think he won't have seen me. Could just make it. Trees around me stiff like soldiers as I jump over rocks, legs catching on a scented pine branch, then ahead I see a bent shape through the trees, ungainly and tearing at the ground. At first I think it's him. But the humped figure is that of Stefan's uncle.

Cicadas sound like rain falling on tin, mechanical and rhythmic.

He's definitely not here. The caravan is empty. Cans of lager on the Formica top, a slight tang of cigarette smoke. Peter said I have eyes like opals, all swirling blues and greens like the picture of the earth from the moon. He never expects me to believe his patter. What we do is just a game to him. We pussy-foot around each other at the tepid water edge. Two in the morning at the water and the sea feels like being caressed by breath. I let him touch me beneath the shore trees like a bad teenager. I let him finger me. I let him open me. He looks like someone I used to know.

First time I saw him was in the street. A local, wearing shorts, long arms held down along his body. A beard, thick black hair, heavily-built, thighs like shot-putters'. Solid on his feet, ponderous even, slouching forward as he walked toward the boats. He stood there smiling. You wanna take it out, he said. I shook my head. His face, appearance and resemblance startled me into silence. Normally I would tell a guy like that to piss off. But I couldn't take my eyes from him and he knew it and kept looking at me and laughing. It wasn't him that I was seeing, not Peter the boatman but someone I once knew. Hypnotized I was, my past in front of me, it seemed, heat rising round him like steam from a diner. Friends say I'm my own worst enemy, that I ask for it. That I ask for trouble. I embrace trouble, they say, like it is your best friend.

Yeah, well, maybe I get bored with hum-drum. I have a friend back in the urban mess of a British city who goes nowhere, does nothing, hides in her house like the world's gonna bite her. And now she's withered like rotten fruit, crushed in the centre and pale around the edges.

So Stefan's not here; that's good, that's good. I settle into the armchair, flop the newspaper around in my hands, then twist a page of a men's magazine and look at the place, littered and scarred. This is home. A place for lies to inhabit like overfriendly guests.

In the dark olive trees as still as sentries. I stand in the doorway of the caravan feet in, feet out, looking at the horizon, looking for the signals of dawn, looking for bent shapes. Quietness suits me; folds round me like skin, like camouflage. Sometimes I just watch the sky gradually transforming, turning bark from lichen green to sooty black, the dry stringy grass to a haven for wild cats, possible wolves, the shapes, the spaces between the trees unfamiliar and sinister with shadows and noise and the sound of the sea down the hill like threatening whispers. Quiet is good, hidden, dark.

Peter is probably snoring, lying on his hairy back with a drink can in his hand like a comfort blanket. Stefan is more than likely with his uncle back at the old house. Least I think he is. His uncle is outside wandering like a blinded Cyclops in the darkness.

It was a long time ago and now I think of you as if a shadow. Or a scent barely recalled but lingering somewhere indefinable in memory; a scent like sweat and lemons and sex – oh yes definitely sex and something of sweetness, something tangy on the tongue and pleasing to the touch. There is no name for it. There is no name for you. There is no name for past.

But you're here regardless, your scent, your past, shadow you, untouchable you.

At first I thought Peter was you. I could barely breathe for thinking it but why would you be here far from your inner-city high living excitement? For a second I dreamed you'd come for me but as I got closer I saw by the falling sullen line of the mouth, by his taller height, by the slightly receding hairline, that it wasn't you. An approximation of you. A facsimile, a dream of you.

Perhaps he is your proxy? If so I am shadowed by them. Proxies of you. Half in substance, in voice, or manners. All shadows. All ghostly. As if someone was practicing to get you right. Or someone liked the prototype so much they thought they'd overpopulate my world with shadows.

Once we lived in a high-rise flat, far over a river. We lived and then fell apart like sides of a jelly mould. The dream split and banality was the end. And I wondered how I had failed and why it had come to this and then we were no more. And you left and I left and no one lived in the flat anymore, no one looked at the river view and dreamed of rowers in darkness.

I am sure Stefan thinks I am pristine. Or close to pristine. I watch at doorways and sneak into the night while Stefan plays chess with his uncle in the old house in the village, and in daylight we lie to each other like old married couples do.

The shape is still there. If that is Stefan's uncle then where is Stefan? And if it's not then who the hell is it? I do nothing and fall onto my saviour bed, in my tight room and dream of high-rise views, of floating out across a city sky on fleshy wings, dive-bombing rowers and cyclists, and further upstream spitting on politicians' bald heads, those black-suited mandarins.

He says he fell asleep in his uncle's kitchen. I don't believe him but say nothing. He grips my arm as I pass him with coffee and paws me like I am his pet. His hair is dark, his eyes a Picasso blue, and his skin tanned dark, olive and glowing. He likes to pull hairs from his nose when no one is looking.

I smile at him. We are so good at pretending. He pretends to want me, and I pretend to enjoy it.

He says his uncle is tired. I say, that isn't surprising.

He looks at me. I am smiling, my teeth baring, like a frightened mink, ready to run. There are no wolves in Greece. We live in a tamed environment. He puts his arm out towards me as if discovering a source of heat.

I saw him out in the grove last night.

You must be mistaken. He looks away, won't look at me.

We're helping with reconstructing his uncle's old house. I collect rocks strewn around the area and bring them back to the shell of the building that looks like rows of teeth stretched up into the sky and along the ground. Walls like biscuit teeth. I make tea. I bring Pepsi. I bring biscuits from the village house. Goats from the mountain wander through. A donkey cries. The sun stares down. And the men work, sweat running off their bodies.

Stefan is a physics student from London. His uncle a farmer who sells honey in the local towns. The beehives, painted blue and striped red, hum like machinery in the olive groves. Remnants of the earthquake, images of one day, of a past that's still the present, brood on the landscape like ghosts, or gravestones.

But really being here is like an extended vacation. Leave off your studies, Nikos said, you're too old for Nobel prizes, come help me with the family house.

Now he complains there's not enough room where the old house was before the earthquake. Too many trees, he says. Too many bloody trees. His Greek accent makes me laugh when he tries to sound like a Londoner, like his nephew.

While Stefan takes a siesta I run to the beach at the bottom of Nikos's land. A small beach, slightly shingled. Mad dogs and Englishmen, I say. The heat is tenacious. And wearing. But in the buoyant sea I am cool and alone.

Sometimes I don't pretend anything and I take off into the mountains, follow my path up the hill, looking for deer tracks. I watch them labouring below me. Summer yachts out in the distance tilt windward around the island. I like the firmness of rocks, the searing shape of them, their hulking mass. And how they let me sit on them, hide behind them. Cypress trees rock in the sea-breeze. A lizard sashays over my feet. I am as still as a setting dog. And hours pass in peace. Sometimes I hear the wild horses come closer and I lie still and feel them breathe over me, their tongues hesitant to lick, their breath steaming out who I am. They are so warm and vibrant and real. Appaloosas, bays and chestnuts. They sniff you out from inside me.

I wonder if Peter looks for me in these mad dog afternoons, waiting for me by the boat, waiting to take me off to some hidden cove. We swam to a beach once. No roads go there. No one to see us. Swimming in the sea as pure as Delphi water, with grey striped fish weaving between our colossus-stance legs.

Every day the house grows. There's so much to do. Nikos talks of Stefan marrying me once the house is built. From this house that the man has built, he says laughing. Stefan looks at me surreptiously like an eager but shy bridegroom. I laugh that he won't want me and Nikos pats Stefan hard on the back as if to say, she there's for the taking. All you have to do is reel her in, noose her like a mountain goat, tie her legs to stop her from escaping to the mountain. Tame what's mad inside her.

I am waiting. The island warmth is sanctuary. The island is a good place to hide. The mountains are high-rises. I love to look from the side, from the top, scrabble up rocks and stare squealing buzzards in the eye. I am mad English. I like heat on my back and in my face. I like to wrestle the sun.

In the night I hear sounds again. Do they think I can't hear them? Do they think I am deaf and stupid? I peel back the curtain. The night is parting gradually, lighting in parts, shifts in the light revealing shapes of density. Two of them, two shapes, huddled, low voices like corralled cows.

I don't hear the other noise first, it's quiet and unobtrusive. I see them together crowding round a tree then backing away slightly and the noise begins. Of whispering, a rapacious noise, voluble like insects. The light changes, becomes stronger. I see feet and hands as the light grows. I see orange and yellow. A tree is alight with fire. Fire is growing up its bark and the shapes are standing back, standing up. I can see them smiling. Or at least Stefan's uncle is. Do they think I sleep?

You used to say I slept like an animal, lightly, alert and ready to run.

I could run. I could skit through the trees like roe deer. Fire could leap from bark to caravan, flash through the window, setting curtains, tables, cushions, papers ablaze. It's not parked that far away.

What the fuck you doing?
  They startle. They look up and grab the shotgun that's beside the truck.
  Just go back inside and mind your own business.
  You can't burn the olive trees down.
  I can, he says, they are mine, they are my property on my land, land I need. Don't you want a big house with everything you need?
  Not at the expense of the trees. I run back to the caravan and grab blankets off the bed, which they reach for as I throw them on the fire, but I'm too nimble for them. I'm in and out before they can stop me. I shout at them, like Monroe in *The Misfits*, all gangly legs and posture with attitude. They back away. Nikos raises his gun towards me, then lowers and pulls on Stefan's arm, she's crazy. Leave her. Don't worry.

I sit there, gripping my knees, rocking back and forth, eyes never leaving the site of the burning, till the smouldering has stopped. Dawn rises timid and thin and my skin chills in the steel-blade light.

He can't chop the trees down, says Stefan next morning. Like strangers, over fresh croissants, we word explanations to each other and nothing sinks in, like oil and water. It's against the law, he says, He can't chop down trees to build on the land.
  But he can burn them down?
  Burning is a force of nature, isn't it? You can't control nature.
  You're both despicable, I stand up, push back the chair from the table, from my half-eaten croissant and toast. You touch those trees again…

And you'll what? He grabs me. It is surprising how a postgrad student, even mature for that, after weeks away from his books, the student desk, the grimy insides of a library or the stiff monotony of a lab stool on his meagre arse, and weeks in the sun, lifting bricks, creating walls, digging drains, can suddenly feel like a different man. I hadn't noticed this before.

I try to shake him off but can't. But I could kick – I have a good kick, I did karate as a teenager. My body remembers the moves as the winter bear remembers the sun. I strike hard, one kick in the shin, another to his groin. I imagine I look sleek, sharply mechanical like the motion of the thrush as it gulps down the worm. There's a yelp and a staggering motion, a quick loosening of the wrist and I twist under his reach, duck down, away and put space between us.

I rub my wrist but he hasn't really hurt me.

High on the mountain I watch the afternoon twist shadows round the shapes of the buildings and car and caravan and the olive trees, and into the carnage Peter walks, calling at the caravan door, calling at the silent building site, kicking the smouldering black stunted remains of a tree, bending down to examine it further. I am silent. I am still. He wanders further, even walks into the caravan where I can't see him but he feels safe enough to be there for some time. I try to imagine what it is he is searching for. He never struck me as the inquisitive jealous type.

I want to fuck Peter, your proxy, on a mountaintop. I want to stand above him and lower myself onto his pliant cock, his belly holding me like you once held me, his hands encircling my arse. Heat on me, sun biting my shoulders, ripening, reading, searing. Flesh for a mountain barbecue. I want to be bronzed and browned and burnished, an edible offering for dusk. I want to work him between my thighs and know we are higher than anything I can see, higher than telephone masts, higher than city high-rise buildings, higher than anyone who can touch us, stop us, pull us apart like fighting cats.

People say I am mad to love a man this long. To love his ghost, to love his image, his memory scent, to close my eyes as I fuck his proxies, his shadows, his doubles, his stand-ins. I am crazing myself.

*

*I close my eyes, Peter's cock inside me, close my eyes and move my
thighs over you like you want, like you want, changing my rhythm so I
clench you harder, pulling up, nearly letting you out of me, ah but
falling back on you and rising your chest rising, your eyes glowing and
crying, moving tighter over you, small movements now, hardly rising at
all but gripping gripping as if I want to hurt you with my grasp, cunt
grip. Then lifting up my legs, and leaning on my feet I fuck you again.
You're astounded, and crying more and someone comes is it you or me
I don't know but the heat is burning and I am gasping and crying to the
air. The mountain air of a Greek island and there is Peter grinning and
I slip off and run barefoot down the mountain so fast he seems unaware
I have gone and down the hill, past the biscuit walls, the caravan and
goats, down the hill to water, to the sea and bury my head bury my head.
You've gone away without me, again.*

Buzzards above, blue-black swimming the air about me. Cypress trees,
the tree of elegy, swaying, and the heat increasing as the sun shifts
around me. I could stay here forever. I could make a home in the rocks
and the trees, a small cabin maybe, but the idea is ridiculous – isn't it?
Escape? To hide and no one to ever find you? And hiding from what?
Is it possible to run from shadows? I want to lose you, the shadow, in a
place where there is no humanity. Or maybe discover you, the real you,
shadowless and vibrant in sunlight, hiding in a pine tree waiting for me
to run past, glance up and see you sitting there, book in hand, reading.
I sleep, dreams and nightmares, seeing shadows from the corner of my
eyes, and the day has gone. Darkness, voices calling my name. I sit up
but say nothing. My nose running as if with a cold. I daren't sneeze. I
daren't even breathe. I can smell them. On the wind they smell of beer
and cigarettes, stale sweat. Men-smell, men-noise, heavy boots. Such
noise they make. Any bird or creature would be flying away from here.
These men know nothing of silence, how to be careful and creeping,
with stealth. Around me it is silent. A crinkly beetle wanders over my
hand and I nearly scream out in surprise. No wind. The trees are
pointed. Sharp cypresses attending upwards into the sky like black-
sooted soldiers.

Then they begin. Not one tree as before but moving to many. They want to be rid of them all. They move quickly but not swiftly – their movements are jumbled, jerky, stumbling. Tripping over stick and rocks. Bent over like sacks. I can do nothing.

The fire begins. Slowly at first, hesitant even, flames moving forward, creeping up the bark, along the grass. Then the breeze lifts up the flames. Once more rapacious it rips through the bark, crumples the green flesh leaves; the embryonic olives, never to see the harvest, crumble, makes ash. Bark disintegrating, like bone cracking. Flames tasting everything

I imagine beetles scurrying, spiders in panic, birds in roost escaping. And who knows what else inhabits these trees. Shadows and ghosts fleeing. I want to cry. Smoke – aromatic and frightening – comes spiralling towards me, pushing me backwards further into the heart of the mountain, the park, the black pine trees, the wild horses. The waiting silence.

But instead I run quickly down the beach side slope of the mountain, finding myself on the village road. All is quiet except the sea hitting the shingle beach and retreating. I think about running to Peter but shadows aren't solid enough in darkness. It's not difficult to untie the boat. Real crime here is unknown.

From the distance of the sea the gathering of flames looks like a massacre. People's lights go on in the village. The shape of the flames change direction as the wind pushes it one way, twists it another, as if playing games. The flames in a mass get bigger and no one does anything. Once out in the open sea I don't know what to do. I sit here feeling the motion of the water pushing me forward and back. The engine cuts. The sound was alien here on the water. Peter will be awake somewhere in his sidestreet house and my shadow will be asleep in his, or are you still with me, a shadow in this boat? Or are you dying in the flames as you wait for me to rescue you?

Metallic light from moon-grey clouds and shadows hiding, like in my head. Orange reflections on a black-grey sea. No siren sounds. The ground is searing and animals run, insects caught in flames as if licked to death by monstrous tongues, deer will be long gone, the wild horses vanishing to the mountainous interior. I wish I was with them. But I am human-smell, girl-smell, you-smell. I would only freak them. I live with phantoms still.

The olive grove burns. The village is awake but uncaring. Light teases the edges of the waves lulling against the boat. Shadows murmur. I sleep until dawn, start up the engines and slowly, like a homecoming, head back to town.

The Summer of Follet and Lilim

1.

A constant roar of cicadas, cops circling, laidback, careful, a swagger, around the outside of the house. Heat, rancid as overripe fruit, as violent as muggers, rises between the suburban trees. Occasionally a car draws up, spots the cops parked at the side of the street – blue lights flashing, white handheld flashlights picking out the haphazard patterns in the rough boards of the white gothic-style house – and draws away as spooked as a suburban fox.

A particular car, guttural throaty raw, comes round twice: at first hesitant, the second time more sure of itself, more intent, moving quickly, carefully upon seeing the cops, checking them out before pulling away with increasing speed, vanishing from sight, unseen by the cops.

But they eye me sitting on the front porch. They watch me suspiciously, despite the fact I am well over the road from the house they have been called to. I am half-hidden in trees and leaves; my feet perched like prize-winning exhibition fish on the rail. I am enjoying the solitude of a sweltering night.

2am. Heat, overwhelming heat in darkness, hotter than an English summer's day, deadening and yet invigorating. The house I inhabit is silent. The cops have guns, and suspicions caught in visceral voices; both are intimidating. The air, though overburdened with heat and sensuality, is way too hot to consider moving, and feels sinister as if violence or the potential for violence is hiding in every front yard and with every footstep coming from the rowdy evening-goers as they saunter down from Massachusetts Avenue. Or is the violence waiting for me inside the sleeping silent walls of my own house? Sometimes I can't judge what will happen next.

I like looking at the street. It makes me feel transparent here in darkness, despite the stares of the cops.

Calm. Flyscreens let the reassuring sounds of stillness escape – a sleeping body snoring, quietly breathing; sometimes the sound of turning sheets sliding over hot skin chafing at sticky covers.

I wonder what the cops want with the house across the way. The size of these guys – like walking mausoleums! The house is empty; its owners have been gone for most of the summer to their cottage in Rockport. Everyone should get out of the city in the summer.

The cops walk the perimeter of the opposite house as if on an exercise in surveillance. Despite their carefree attitude they appear intent, even shark-like in their quest and hunt. This mechanical blindness to anything but their duty is frightening, like the forward relentless motion of an engine.

I hide in the bushes, covering myself with the smell of sycamore leaves and potted basil. They continue to look my way as if alerted to movement or the sense of watching eyes. I can't leave; placing my feet on the green painted boards of the front porch deck would ignite the glare of the automatic security light, and wake him inside. The other body in the house sleeps peacefully. Voice silent, I open my mouth. I close my mouth, I go to shout to the cops and yet...

The body inside the room turns in his sleep. The cicadas stop briefly, though the peepers take up the call. The cops cross the road, look up at me, standing there in the centre of the road as if mesmerized, as if expecting the falling shadow of a cat-burglar to crash upon them.

In the silence the body inside snores, a car rushes by, pumping out dub reggae, and I think it'll wake him, and suddenly I am more scared of that than of the cops looking at me.

Follet says nothing when he wakes in the morning. He tumbles from the bed not realizing I have been missing from his side half the night, grabs tissues and his contacts from the bedside table and vanishes into the bathroom. I watch him from the corner seat. He hasn't noticed I'm there nor I'm not there. I'm not sure this is a good thing or not. To be ignored – isn't that the worst thing in the world?

2.

My pattern, now that Lilim-the smiler has come, is to wander the porch and the gravel gardens with its climbable trees in which to hide, and its tall blue flowers to sniff. One tree is shaped like it has been windblown eastwards. Its shape fascinates me: it looks as if to be running away from itself.

At the garden gate I stand, looking out. Sometimes passing people smile at me and I smile back or run into the house in case he sees me or she sees me. In this house of dreams and memories I have trapped myself. My gaolers are but the catalysts for my own desires. Lilim has her side of the house and I have mine. He moves between, heavy-footed, trailing his preferences like a long exotic cape.

Days pass. Sometimes Follet lets me shuffle along the porch in daylight while he stands behind the flyscreen, smoking, watching. He watches the house. He listens for the ring of the phone. The phone is in the hall. I haven't access to the hall. In spaces when he is away from my side, or when I sit on the rocking chair at night, eyes closed, I bring to mind what is forbidden. He tries to bind my mind like he does my wrists and feet and my duty here. But he cannot tie down what is already inside of me. I remember the start of the summer. When we were alone, before Lilim came. Heat overawed me. As did he. It is

3.

almost as if he were a dream, a ghost, a figment conjured out of need. Sometimes I wonder if what we had was real at all. If walking through an evening square in the city – white fairy lights round the trees, young people lounging on benches, as the whole world, under that light sky in that despotic heat, was gobbling on ice-cream to cool down and for sensual pleasure – was ever real or just something I'd seen in a film. Us holding hands, us joking and teasing each other, him putting on silly voices and embarrassing me into pretending to run away. I recall us sitting there commenting on the nationality of a dark-haired girl beside us talking rapidly into her cell phone in a language neither of us could recognize. We wondered if she was Greek or Romanian – she had the colouring, skin the hue of a coconut shell – lightly browned, frazzled by the sun.

And when I slept beside him he felt so real, so absolutely inhabiting time and space as if he had always done so, and always would, like granite on a Cornish moor. I would feel him breathing and the very sound of him filled the room and filled me and made me know I was there. I too was as solid as granite, even maybe as shiny as crystalline rock, or flecked with gold like lapis lazuli or shiny and as precious as cornelian or amber. We had so short a time together; so transitory and yet so sky-splintering.

He, as he was, his shape, his reality, is nebulous to me now, as untouchable as mist. Yet his form once walked around a square, feet finding concrete as soft as over-cooked pasta. I would walk past a bank and see him laughing. I would walk past a diner and feel his hand in mine, but a half-formed half-imagined hand – like something x-rayed my mind has to cover with flesh and white-pink skin to recreate as real. I recreate him nightly, daily when he doesn't realize it. I recreate him as I lie in the bath; I recreate him in my mind when I eat or cook or when pulling out a Pepsi bottle from the cupboard, and I smile as I form him beside me. I am like Pygmalion fashioning my ideal from memories rather than clay. He is as real as the sky but as distant as air.

I have pictures of him, of us, as he was, as I was and it seems so real and yet nowhere that could have existed. Not now. Not knowing what I know now. I see us on beaches, snatching a minute's breather in a crowded city, eating fries crowned like the Pearly kings and queens. I feel us in heat, sweating, heat oozing from us, soaking every pore. I feel his forehead as I cleanse him with a tissue, fiddling with the Celtic cross hanging around his neck, I see him lying on grass under fire from a sprinkler's gaze. I am lying with him. We look like lovers. Faces pass us and they smile because we look like lovers and we look happy and such happiness in the city is rare where people hardly take time away from the minutiae of their existence to revel in their potential for sublimity.

We were something out of time; we were freeze-frames in a blur of flashed film. We were creatures fashioned from our imaginations. We were as precious as breathing.

I do not cry. He who I had is gone from me. Why should I cry? It cannot have been real; I am not convinced. Memories are as vague as fog. If I'd known how fleeting it would all be I would have never let go of his arm, or let him out of my sight. I would have taken him far away from here before ever agreeing to stay. I would have looked at him and looked at him and taken in even more, so that his face would be even more familiar than my own blood-flecked eyes reflected at me, that his smell would have intermingled with mine, that standing in a bookstore it would be him I'd be peering at intently, not the array of books on New England bird life tumbling over the *Your Shape Diet* books. I wouldn't have left him while I walked to the water's edge, picking up shells and hedonistically revelling in the coolness of the ocean, staring at the families, the planes overhead and the birds circling me like prey. I would have dragged him with me, not leaving him on the border of sand and water, staring at my distant shape and my movements. I would have taken his arms and dragged him – his whole frame, taking his palm in mine, burning his wrist with the force of me. I would be like Hercules pulling him to me. What nights I would have, never closing my eyes as I breathed him in through dilated pupils, my scarified irises and bloodshot sclera sizzled by staring.

The spaces of the walls of the house notice the absence of what I felt as love; they mock me with their cavernous resentment. Spaces grow.

Shapes move across the road; then the sudden roar of returning people high on laughter and freedom. Lights flicker at the opposite house. The telephone doesn't ring. The stultifying breeze tumbles through the slats in the blinds. A car pulls up. My porch security light snaps on. The man who stands before me is not the man of my memories.

4.
The air around me is hot, like it's been for weeks, as the cab drivers

complained to me when I first got here, as if they expected me not to have noticed, blasting out their air-conditioning while slumped back in low-slung leather modified seats, hunting through the city streets for quick cuts and lazy pedestrians mollified by the overwhelming heat. The city moves still but slowly slowly, lumbering like over-burdened beasts through the day and into slightly cooler night. While I stand at the window the city around me shuffles forward, vehicles honking, stopping and starting at traffic lights, engines wheezing, people shouting, TV screens flickering. Someone across the street has a TV screen the size of a cinema. Gandalf is battling with Balrog in the mines of Moira. Gandalf's grey beard and heavy lined face is visible from here. The bridge collapses and for a moment there is pure terror.

There is something going on at the house opposite; it is almost as if they are watching us – watching the changing movements across blinded windows, the changing shapes. Lights go on and off. Drapes move, blinds swish up and down as if lifted by a mechanical pulley.

Lilim is beside me. She says, "He was never really yours." I try to turn away but she grabs me – she is long thin, straight boyish figure but with eyes as large as manhole covers. When she walks she thrusts her body forward, her arse backwards. She reminds me of someone who has spent too many formative years horse riding. Sometimes I can even smell the aroma of leather and sweat coming from her – the smell of a tackroom. "I was always here," she says. She likes it when he's absent.

Sometimes I think it's a voice in my head. Sometimes I think I've made all these people up. Sometimes I think I should run to the sofa and throw myself under the covers and never come out.

Once I had a child and it was taken away.

Once I had a dream and it was exorcised.

Now I have walls, pine floors, a sophisticated kitchen stocked with rare European gin, Italian reds and French white and liqueurs with fancy titles, and in the fridge – a fridge with an ice crusher and ice box – is rocket salad and tiny cherry tomatoes in a Japanese wooden bowl. On the fridge are Simpson cartoon magnets. I move them around when I have nothing else to do.

Her voice comes again. Sometimes I try to push it away. But I see her and she looks so innocent, as if what I have thought about her cannot be true. She says, "You're playing me." This always surprises me because I always feel tossed and flung like a toy every time she touches me, every time he touches me. I say, "It wasn't meant to be like this."

I rush from the room then, hives forming like welts behind my ears, needing the solidity of the street, needing to see those monstrous cops circling the building opposite. I need to feel, to reach out, touch them and they will help me even though they do not know who I am. White chargers in navy uniform.

But I never do. I'm sure I know the way out of this but I cannot take it.

It wasn't like this at first. It was simple and light and sweet. Whenever we saw each other, spoke to each other, it felt like it was meant to be. We thought we knew what we were doing.

I say to her, "He said you didn't mind. He hinted it was over."

She laughs. "He lies. Do you think I will ever let him go? Do you think he is capable of ever not knowing me?"

5.

When Follet makes love to me at night, I can feel her in his mind. She never used to be there, or at least she never was so strong. Who is the more ridiculous, the buyer or the seller of a dream?

She stays away then, but I can hear her crying in her own darkness.

In afternoons, when the house is hotter than a Turkish steam room, they argue, always scrabbling and discussing the same old stuff. Going round and round, her asking why do you have to have her, him saying I do. Her saying I feel betrayed, him saying, I'm sorry, what can I do? They argue like this when she comes home with groceries, when he buys himself a magazine, when he looks at me. He tells her she could leave. She weeps, bent over like a willow. Light slices through the slants of the blinds.

Sometimes he walks into the room and I shiver. He sees me glowing and walks away. Deliberately, coldly, smiling to himself. I'm left glowing to an empty room. I can feel myself dissipating, shivering alive and dead, shivering to keep hold onto some resemblance of reality. This glow is addictive. With the heat and his touch, the house, my life the people are more intangible, yet his touch is the only thing that gives me hope.

Then he returns and makes me open my legs for him to feast in admiration upon the beautiful geometry of my cunt before touching me gently on shoulders, neck, between my breasts, down my stomach, my thighs, backs of my calves, turning me over, soles of my feet. I can hardly bear the lightness, the exquisite moment of touch, the anticipation of where on my body will he touch me next, how light will it be and can I stand it when I want more and more and I always want more and wanting more he will not give it me.

6.
Different cops now, different shapes in a different Ford, bringing with them more heat, as they circle, as their parked vehicle floods the air with fumes. Are they watching this house? Or over the road? It is now impossible to tell. The room behind me is full of strawberries and kiwi and grapes and cream from fat cakes.

7.
Follet and Lilim over me goading me on, me arching my body towards them as taut as if on gossamer thread. The smell of incense, the touch of silk. She's at my head looking into my eyes as he thrusts his tongue between my legs. They would feed me with words, lie me down like a baby upon blankets of dreaming words. Words as plump as a goose feather comforter. Words from their mouths sneak around my body, settling between my legs like his hand at night, oozing on my breasts, soften me, ease me – these words have dreams in them. These words lift souls, they fatten me.

Then comes their flesh, creeping over me like honey slipping down my throat, creeping into crevices of my body. Follet touches me now with

Lilim's guidance and encouragement. She has seen its power. Flesh, skin, gentle, hard, blood mingling, cells merging into cells, atoms unsplitting. He presses his fingers into my thighs as she stands looking. The power of watching, of touching vicariously. He and I out there lingering in the mind of each other. Like angels on collision course.

Lilim nourishes me with his love.

But then, just when it is perfect, she pulls away, she says, "I can't, I'm scared, I can't be here, this is not me, if you love me you will come away, you will give her up." And she leaves and he cries, turning away from me back into his head.

I ache then. For their absence. For his distance, and such a feeling of emptiness sets up inside me. I had their voices, their flesh, their words to keep me full, now all I can feel is absence – the feeling of what was once there and no longer is. An ex-presence, an ex-fullness. The opposite of full. These moments of down waste me like nothing I have ever felt. Nothing I can put into my body nor my mind can replace it.

8.

The cops come. Always they are at the opposite house looking in. Sometimes I feel their presence acutely and want to run to them, take them by their hands and make them push me like a criminal into the back of their car. Their arms are lifting up, stretching out, guns pointing to the house. I see them from behind closed blinds, lifting a tiny sliver to gain view of the world outside this house, the prison I have trapped myself in. My voice is absent. I can no more call for them than I can jump over the roofs and across the ocean. I am barely able to walk to the kitchen. How hot it is. I am sated with smiles.

I am no longer bound to the house. They no longer care where I go – so sure are they of my steadfastness, and my fidelity, so sure are they that their magic has worked. They can see how little I argue, how accommodating I am to their every need, how little I demand that I should demand; that I am bound as if physically chained. I have pledged my very cells to them, to their love of me. I am unvoiced. Days pass alone but I am waiting and I have memories to recreate. I look out the window, at cops, at my eastward tree, still bent towards the ocean, and at passing strangers. But mostly I sleep and wait. They always come for me again, bringing morsels, caresses and words and thoughts and dreams on silver platters; though they attend to me less regularly than they once did. I don't know where they go once they are away from here. Having possessed me they tire of me.

Sometimes Follet wakes me, entering the room quietly, and shoves his cock into me and half-dreaming I come and wonder when I wake if it was real.

9.
Late afternoon, day vanishing into dusk, the cicadas impatient for the sun to go. The day feels wasted and old. The house is empty. I sense emptiness, but I still cannot move. I am trussed and bound as if in a parlour of cobwebs. The sun is going. The sky is pink, red, orange, blue takes over, then dark blue, darker blue so dark it is like emptiness. The trees silhouette. I do nothing but wait. I sit naked and wait; I touch myself fruitlessly and wait. I listen for sounds. The sky is dark. The sounds of cicadas, passing cars, spooky creaks in the wooden floors, the repetitive whirr of the fridge so loud, like a plane. I am waiting. I am here. Here. Waiting. Thinking. Feel how my skin tingles at the thought of him. I have to keep thinking of him; remembrances, memories, create him from visions.

The cops return, banging the door with malice, shouting and demanding entry but I cannot say a word. I have no voice. It is too much to even open my eyes into slivers of light, and motions across space. Everything is heavy and languorous but my binds feel tight and yet flimsy. I could break away. I could wriggle and break away. Heat increases every time I move. When I move I feel scared. So I sit still. Still stiller. Naked in light. Streetlights through the blinds. The room once spacious is close now. Heat around me. Heat, slivers of light, cool floor. Sit upright; sit straight, heat on my skin, coolness from the floor hitting my clit. The cops shouting, inquisitive shapes slash through the dusted light. To them this is an empty house.

They will come back for me, won't they? They won't leave me hanging, the words, the dreams, and transcendental hopes, these tortured bones that I am, the heated days and sweaty nights, rivulets of sweat, a dish for cicadas, picking at my words eating in languorous motion, slow slow, hardly breathing, door banging. Still still, movements my movements my movements.

More quality fiction from Elastic Press

☐ The Virtual Menagerie	Andrew Hook	SOLD OUT
☐ Open The Box	Andrew Humphrey	SOLD OUT
☐ Second Contact	Gary Couzens	SOLD OUT
☐ Sleepwalkers	Marion Arnott	SOLD OUT
☐ Milo & I	Antony Mann	SOLD OUT
☐ The Alsiso Project	Edited by Andrew Hook	SOLD OUT
☐ Jung's People	Kay Green	SOLD OUT
☐ The Sound of White Ants	Brian Howell	SOLD OUT
☐ Somnambulists	Allen Ashley	SOLD OUT
☐ Angel Road	Steven Savile	SOLD OUT
☐ Visits to the Flea Circus	Nick Jackson	SOLD OUT
☐ The Elastic Book of Numbers	Edited by Allen Ashley	SOLD OUT
☐ The Life To Come	Tim Lees	SOLD OUT
☐ Trailer Park Fairy Tales	Matt Dinniman	SOLD OUT
☐ The English Soil Society	Tim Nickels	£5.99
☐ The Last Days of Johnny North	David Swann	SOLD OUT
☐ The Ephemera	Neil Williamson	SOLD OUT
☐ Unbecoming	Mike O'Driscoll	£6.99
☐ Photocopies of Heaven	Maurice Suckling	SOLD OUT
☐ Extended Play	Edited by Gary Couzens	£6.99
☐ So Far, So Near	Mat Coward	£5.99
☐ Going Back	Tony Richards	£5.99
☐ That's Entertainment	Robert Neilson	£5.99
☐ The Cusp of Something	Jai Clare	£5.99

All these books are available at your local bookshop or can be ordered direct from the publisher. Indicate the number of copies required and fill in the form below.

Name_____
(Block letters please)

Address_____

Send to Elastic Press, 85 Gertrude Road, Norwich, Norfolk, NR3 4SG.
Please enclose remittance to the value of the cover price plus: £1.50 for the first book plus 50p per copy for each additional book ordered to cover postage and packing. Applicable in the UK only.

While every effort is made to keep prices low, it is sometimes necessary to increase prices at short notice. Elastic Press reserve the right to show on covers and charge new retail prices which may differ from those advertised in the text or elsewhere.

Want to be kept informed? Keep up to date with Elastic Press titles by writing to the above address, or by visiting www.elasticpress.com and adding your email details to our online mailing list.

Elastic Press: Winner of the British Fantasy Society Best Small Press award 2005

Previously from Elastic Press

That's Entertainment by Robert Neilson

What if John Lennon had been kicked out of the Beatles? What if Elvis' twin brother had survived? What if we could go back in time to give reality TV a historical perspective? What if the Pope was Irish, a gambler, and needed to bet on a dead cert? In Neilson's science fiction, fantasy lives just around the corner from reality.

A great new talent in storytelling – Anne McCaffrey

Forthcoming from Elastic Press

Other Voices by Andrew Humphrey

Andrew Humphrey follows up his acclaimed first collection, "Open The Box", with another twelve stories of loss and abandonment, fear and greed. Moving through the genres of urban horror, science fiction, crime and slipstream, Humphrey examines the effects of the fantastic upon the personal, whether through future dystopias, a missing child, climatic change, or repeated infidelity.

An original and unique vision – Eric Brown

For further information visit:
www.elasticpress.com

Extended Play:
The Elastic Book of Music

What does music do for you? Is it an art form, mood enhancer, or just something to jump around to? From the orchestra pit to the mosh pit music inspires our lives, is universal and personal, futuristic yet primordial. As the soundtrack trigger to a thousand memories it can be seductive yet soulful, energetic and prophetic. But the immediacy of music has rarely been exploited within literature. Until now...

With fiction from Marion Arnott, Becky Done, Andrew Humphrey, Emma Lee, Tim Nickels, Rosanne Rabinowitz, Philip Raines, Tony Richards, Nels Stanley, and Harvey Welles.

Accompanying the stories, songwriters comment on how fiction has influenced their music, with contributions from JJ Burnel, Gary Lightbody, Chris Stein, Sean "Grasshopper Mackowiak, Lene Lovich, Chris T-T, Rebekah Delgado, Tall Poppies, jof owen, and Iain Ross.

www.elasticpress.com

We Want Your Stories!

Elastic Press is currently open for submissions to "Subtle Edens: The Elastic Book of Slipstream" to be edited by Allen Ashley, the award-winning editor of our previous anthology, "The Elastic Book of Numbers".

Full guidelines can be viewed on our website.

"Subtle Edens - The Elastic Book of Slipstream" - anthology.
Allen Ashley requires:
Original Slipstream stories up to 5000 words.
Payment: via Contributor copy / copies.
Response Time: 8 weeks.
Opening date: 1st June 2007.
Closing date: 29 February 2008.
Send "Disposable" hard copy manuscripts to:
Allen Ashley, Editor - "Subtle Edens", 110 Marlborough Road, Bounds Green, London N22 8NN, England.

All email enqiuries to Allen at:

editorsubtleedens@hotmail.co.uk